Criminal Capers

Nigel Scott

Brown Bear Books

Published by:
Brown Bear Books
Dial Post
Horsham
West Sussex
RH13 8NX

A CIP catalogue record for this book is available from the British Library.

Printed and bound in Great Britain.

ISBN 0 9536077 2 0

Atween the wet ground and the dry
The gold of Fairnilee doth lie!
Andrew Lang

Contents

For Denis, Joan Deitch, Auntie Marie, Sara Bowers and Rosie, John C. and John U. (the experts), Jeremy (at Pretty's Garage), Val and Jeff Burrows (not forgetting Brock the Pooch), Lesley, Mrs Sharp and of course 'Typist Extraordinaire' Mum

A Grain of Evidence

Injured during an armed robbery at a *Sub-Post Office in Tulse Hill, Frank Donaldson, then a detective and member of the famous Flying Squad with men under him was callously shot in the back while protecting a young woman with her pram. The bullet caused permanent damage to the spine, subsequently leaving him paralysed from the waist down.

Every disabled person must be courageous and objective to some degree but what drew me towards Frank, in particular, as a nurse at Stoke Mandeville Hospital (apart from the fact it turned out we were both widowers) was a shared interest in the causes and detection of crime plus a real love of flying ... flying radio controlled model aircraft that is!

Although at times, over sensitive, introspective and naturally uncertain of the future, Frank often confided to me that despite his injuries, the outrageous prospect often tempted him of setting up a Private Detective Agency on the South Coast.

Frank proposed I quit the nursing profession altogether and we form a business partnership – well, I was fed up with the pay and wanted a bit of a change.

The same month we moved into our little ground floor flat in Hove, a particularly ingenious and memorable crime was perpetrated on the London Underground.

It happened during the evening rush-hour a week before Christmas, a train left Hampstead Underground Station and was entering the tunnel when a phone call was relayed to the Central London Railway Control

*Forest Row Sub-Post Office

7

Centre and Fire Brigade Headquarters ... someone was apparently lying on the conductor rail in the tunnel between Hampstead and Golders Green Stations.

The track circuit in that section of the underground system was instantly switched off and emergency procedures activated.

Because of automatic signalling the next south-bound train at Golders Green Station did not proceed. The north-bound train, now accelerating at a speed of thirty five miles an hour, came to a halt mid-way through the tunnel at a red light. Barely had fire-crew and ambulance personnel had a chance to trudge along that section of track, brandishing their acetylene lamps and stretcher when, what passengers on the stationary Golders Green bound tube assumed was a friendly blind man with long woolly ginger beard and sunglasses, wearing navy blue woollen mittens, mackintosh and trilby hat, tapped his way down the central gangway of the middle car. He quite unexpectedly pointed a revolver at the guard's head and in a squeaky voice asked if the pneumatically controlled doors might be opened as he suffered from claustrophobia and was in need of some fresh air!

Operated by push-button, the doors parted. Afterwards a loud whistle was heard from the front of the train. The blind man, after hand-cuffing the guard to his control panel, wished everybody a Merry Christmas and jumped down on to the line – only to vanish into the musty gloom of the tunnel.

What was going on? Meanwhile a man in a bowler, wearing a black balaclava, jumped into the second car and again at gun-point, snatched a pig-skin brief case belonging to Mr. Gregory Cohen, a regular commuter on the line. The brief case happened to contain two million quid's worth of De Beers rough-cut diamonds. Mr. Cohen, being a dealer in precious stones with offices at Hatton Gardens.

Both tunnel entrances, one at Hampstead the other, Golders Green Station, were sealed off a couple of minutes after the original emergency phone call was logged.

No one, apart from personnel such as British Transport Police, ambulance and fire crew were seen leaving or entering the tunnel. Subsequently a kind of hybrid 'Guy Fawkes' dummy, decapitated at neck and ankles, was discovered slumped across the rails in the tunnel... the trousers and jumper stuffed with old newspaper and straw.

Items of disguise corresponding exactly to passengers' description of our friendly blind man and his accomplice, the 'Whistler', including sunglasses, bowler hat, black balaclava and woolly ginger beard were later found amongst some rubbish at the bottom of a wastepaper bin on the north-bound platform of Hampstead Station.

Police were satisfied that while inside the tunnel the gem thieves, donning yet another disguise, posed as emergency personnel and slipped out using the lift, making their escape in a taxi at the station entrance above ground.

Barely had the popular tabloids, much to Scotland Yard's chagrin, trumpeted front page headlines like 'The Perfect Crime Committed on the Underground' along with pages devoted to matrix diagrams, informative 'Cut Away' plans and isometric reconstruction of the tunnel showing the infamous section between Hampstead and Golders Green. (Something not altogether lost to readers being the fact that about 300 yards North of the station, the Hampstead Line runs no less than 250 feet below the crest of Hampstead Heath), when a couple of days later Mr. Cohen received, at his Hatton Gardens office, a parcel containing the missing rough-cut diamonds – the parcel sent through regular Post Office channels from Brighton so someone had evidently got cold feet.

But who was the *Criminal Mastermind* behind such an audacious enterprise and how had the operation been planned? Acting on a hunchFrank decided to go to London and solve the mystery.

We owned a Messerschmitt 'Tiger' Bubble Car. Being mechanically minded Frank had replaced the engine of the Bubble Car with a Yamaha Motorcycle 750 cc engine, to considerably increase the speed and adapted the brakes, clutch and throttle to be hand-operated from levers behind the steering wheel. The drivers seat revolved round to face the canopy door to enable easy access for a disabled person.

Being the Christmas Holiday there was little traffic on the roads and we arrived at Hampstead Village around ten o'clock. Frank drove up Heath End Hill and parked the Bubble Car in the forecourt of a pub he had wanted us to take a look at.

The 'Bull and Bush' was half-timbered with black and red checked brickwork. The pub overlooked acres of open space, situated north of the city.

Scaffolding had been erected around the steep pitched roof and along the back extension. The place was boarded up – tables and benches stacked up in the beer garden.

There was a notice pinned to one of the lower storey windows:

> *'A Merry Christmas to all our customers.*
> *Closed until renovations completed.*
> *Sorry for inconvenience caused.*
>
> *R. Lion (Landlord)*
>
> *Our Annual New Year's Dinner and Dance*
> *will be held at 'The Castle'.*
> *Tickets from Mr Batley.'*

"We'll have to find somewhere else to have a pint," I said. "What about the 'Castle'?"

Frank was not listening. He pointed at a group of tall, silver poplars.

"I'm a little uneasy about something," he said, adjusting the focus on a pair of handy binoculars – peering through the glasses.

"Are we being followed or what?" I asked.

"No, nothing dramatic like that! It's that diamond robbery on the Northern Line, Harry – I've got an old copper's hunch! Hello – we've got company."

Frank put his binoculars away and free-rolled his wheelchair down the grassy bank. Striding amongst the furze beyond the tall poplars, was someone beating this way and that, with a long stick wearing a deer-stalker and travelling cape, smoking a yellow meersham pipe.

As we approached, he suddenly caught sight of us and looked a bit embarrassed.

"Frank Donaldson," my pal called out, throwing his blue and white Seagulls Supporters Club scarf over one shoulder.

"Sid Ramsbottom" the chap shouted back.

On closer inspection, far from being lean and hawk-featured like Sherlock Holmes, he was plumpish with wavy blonde hair!

"Member 'out Sherlock Holmes Society of London – bit of an amateur but I 'as a go any'ow." He held out his gloved hand and Frank shook it warmly.

By coincidence, he came from Brighton and had travelled (with his bicycle) down by train from the South Coast to Victoria.

"I think you're on the right track, young man," Frank said, with a grin. "This was my line of enquiry – exactly."

Frank intimated to the strange Ferro-concrete dome shaped structure situated some yards away in the undergrowth, covered by sprawling bracken.

What was it – some sort of hide used by parties of bird watchers – an old flak gun emplacement?

"That's 'ow they got t'platform level." The Sherlockian went over and stood beside it – puffing furiously on his pipe despite the fact that it had gone out!

"The ventilator…" sighed Frank.

"Aye – that's right," replied Ramsbottom, who spoke with a strong Yorkshire accent. "I've knocked some of crap out t'way so yer'll be able to get wheelchair in 'ere wi'out too much difficulty."

We edged forward. I pushed Frank's wheelchair across the thick, tussocky grass until we reached the perimeter of the concrete dome.

Ramsbottom chewed on the stem of his pipe thoughtfully.

"You know railway company originally built t'section o' line that runs directly beneath 'ere in 1906 – like."

"You're a railway buff," Frank said, brushing some bracken and leaves from the dome with his mitten.

"Used to be called 'Charin' Cross, Euston 'n 'ampstead Railway' – didn't yer know that, Mr. Donaldson?"

"Take a lesson out of Holmes' book – don't stuff your mind with a lot of bloody useless facts!" suggested Frank, tartly.

"Listen – what I want to know as an ex-copper is whether there's any footprints … proper evidence!"

"I've n'owt been able to see any," the Yorkshireman admitted. "T'weather's so mucky of late – I did find this – though."

Pulling off his glove, Sid dug deep into his pocket and pulled out a many faceted old sparkler – the tiny diamond nestled snugly in the palm of his hand.

"Proof, if any wer't needed!" he said, pompously.

Frank wasn't particularly impressed.

"Where's the entrance to this bloody concrete dome, young man?"

"Keep moving round t'her left of t'dome and you'll come t'riveted door – 'bout four feet tall like – course I took ole Sherlock's methods to heart – examined brass padlock carefully wi' magnifying lens – didn't I."

"Full marks – any smudges, scratches or indentations?"

"Sod all, mate!"

"The padlock was probably changed. The brass looks remarkably untarnished considering how exposed we are."

Frank nudged his spectacles. "The clever clogs who planned this robbery was meticulous to the last detail. I'd reckon they sheared through the old padlock with cutters and simply replaced it with another one after resurfacing with the stolen gems."

"Funny irnt'it – when I come 'ere early in t'morning on't bike I'd swear now't ad tred on't grass – looked like nobody'd bin' near the thing for't donkey's years."

"Must have been dark."

"Oh, I 'ad a powerful torch alright," Ramsbottom insisted. "Only started to tread al't over grass when you lot turned 'oop int' Bubble Car."

"I'm still not clear on one thing," I said, blowing clouds of freezing air. "Why should they build a ventilator here in the first place, Frank – what's there to ventilate?"

"You thick or summat?" the Yorkshireman said, sarcastically. "Look Harry" Frank explained "when this section of the Northern Line was built, plans were laid for five stations – Chalk Farm, Belsize Park, Hampstead, Bull and Bush – named after that boarded up pub up there – and Golders Green which was only a fringe village then.

What we've got here, and I'm sure young Ramsbottom will agree with me, is one of the original 12 feet diameter working shafts retained to serve as an air extraction duct for the station beneath.

They'd already got round to building galleries to house the ozonisers and other equipment necessary to purify the air when the London Electric Railway Company decided to shelve the project. Work never got completed and the Bull and Bush Underground Station disappeared into the annals of railway oblivion. You can just about make out the old abandoned platforms, when you go past it on the tube."

"The station must be an awful long way down, Frank?"

"Granted, but there are no doubt galvanised iron ladders leading to the central fairing where the fan would have normally been installed a hundred feet or so below the ground and deep sunk staircase wells after that."

"What if gem thieves 'ad climbing experience – they'd 'ave ropes 'n graplin' 'ooks t'scale large sections of t'shaft?" proposed the Sherlockian filling his pipe.

"Bit too fiddly for my money!" Frank poked about in the grass with a lengthy piece of twig. "I reckon they simply used what was already there – ladders and steps. The ventilator was nearing completion when work stopped – remember?"

Sid Ramsbottom leaned against the concrete dome, pipe clenched between his teeth, twiddling his thumbs – watching the sleet settle on the ground. Frank leaned over and scooped up a handful of brick coloured sandy substance from the base of the concrete dome. He let the stuff slip through his fingers and grunted.

"Harry – where does that diamond dealer, Cohen, live?"

"Golders Green – that's what the Mirror said."

"What was the road?"

"Hoop Lane – there was a picture of his house." I took out the crumpled tabloid and showed him.

"Well, that's a coincidence – Mike Viney, of all people lives in Golders Green."

"Viney – whos'ee?" asked Ramsbottom, dismissively.

"Ever heard of the Viney-Marks chain of jewellery shops – South Coast Branches at Worthing, Brighton, Eastbourne – as well as Camden, Ealing, Kilburn …? They're all over North London. Got that diamond handy, Mr Ramsbottom … I'd like to take a closer look at it … if I may."

Frank borrowed our friend's magnifying lens to examine it minutely. "Listen Harry, we'll need a BT Telephone Directory. I've got to check some addresses. What about you Mr Ramsbottom? Fancy a nice Boxing Day lunch at 'The Castle'? Northerners do celebrate Boxing Day – don't they?" he laughed raucously.

"Aye – we do that!" said the Yorkshireman striding through the furze towards his bicycle. "I've a feeling you're on ta summat Mr. Donaldson – 't 'games afoot' as Holmes might have said!" Fastening the flaps of his deerstalker beneath his chin to fend off the worst of the sleet, the Yorkshireman leapt on his bicycle and peddled towards the pub.

"Just stick that on the trailer." I shouted pushing Frank for all I was worth towards the pub forecourt. The concrete dome of the ventilator in the distance now covered with a light dusting of snow. "Ours is the old Jerry Bubble Car – should just squeeze you in the front!"

Well, according to the phone book this Mike Viney not only lived in the same road as the diamond dealer, Cohen, but was his nextdoor neighbour as well. After a nice lunch at the 'Castle' we drove the Bubble Car across Hampstead to Golders Green.

If Cohen's house at No. 43 Hoop Lane could best be described as a 'Colonial Mansion' – rather similar to one of those plantation houses in the film 'Gone with the Wind'... Viney's at No. 40 was more 'Tudor Manor House' – that's to say herringbone brickwork and big chimney stacks. A Christmas tree, festooned with baubles and tinsel and blinking fairy lights stood in each driveway... Viney's a bit taller and the more impressive of the two.

The front door of No. 40 was opened by a girl wearing high heels and a calf-length black skirt. She looked very pretty and I presume thought – what with Frank in his wheelchair and us looking like a pair of prize goons, that we were from some disabled Servicemen's Charity, come to waggle a collection tin under her nose – mind you, it was probably Sid Ramsbottom wearing that tweedy Sherlock Holmes get-up that made her jaw drop.

"Is Mike there by any chance?" Frank's friendly manner seemed to reassure her.

"Dad's in the living room." She gave my pal a kind and over sympathetic smile ... the kind Frank detested. It translated 'Poor old cripple'.

"Could I have a word with your dad?"

The girl spent what seemed like a bloody age running her fingers through her blonde, spiky hair.

"I'll fetch him for you, Mister...?"

"Oh Donaldson – Frank Donaldson."

Presently Mike Viney came to the door clutching a dog. The poodle looked like a piece of miniature topiary dyed pink – it bared its fangs and growled menacingly.

"Yeah – what can I do for you boys?" he asked, stroking the dog's woolly head.

"Diamonds!" Frank folded his arms and waited for the blue-touch paper to smoulder.

"Why not talk to one of my managers – what are you after … watches, rings? We've got nice discount prices at all my branches until the end of January – try your luck at the sales!"

He looked (as well he might) a bit put out and was about to slam the door in our faces.

"Uncut diamonds, Mr Viney! Two million quids worth! Went walkies on the London Underground."

"Oh the robbery on the Northern Line – that's old hat now – isn't it! Who are you, anyway? Reporters – I see you've brought along the great detective –" he chuckled – "Sherlock Holmes … is this some sort of stunt – what paper are you from? 'People', 'News of the World' – get lost before I chuck a stick of dynamite under that wheelchair of yours.

That'd make good copy wouldn't it – sell a few papers!"

The poodle was barking. I was severely tempted to strangle it! Luckily Viney's daughter came to the door and snatched the animal.

"Do be quiet, bootiful Bootles!" She cradled the thing – rocking it back and forth like a cherub faced little baby.

Frank, meanwhile, reached into his pocket for an envelope and opened it out. There was a rust-coloured sandy substance, mixed with a bit of what looked like dirt.

"Ballast, Mr Viney – one of your sacks must have been damaged when your balloon either landed or made its ascent from the top of that Ferro-concrete ventilator!"

"Good God – you know!" he gauped, pushing his daughter back inside – "How?"

"I recall reading an article in the Mirror about that flight of yours with a couple of leggy fashion models in a balloon, piloted by your brother from Eastbourne to Brighton sea-front as a stunt to publicise the Viney-Marks chain of jewellers, couple of years back! Now according to Directory Enquiries, your brother, Richard, lives in Brighton – well, that's a bit useful because the package sent to the diamond dealer at Hatton Garden was identified as having been post-marked 'Western Road Post Office, Brighton'."

"Oh gawd, I think you boys had better come in… I don't want old Cohen overhearing this … he normally takes his dogs out for a walk about now."

We were shown into a big living room ponging of delicious Havana cigars with all the luxury of deep pile carpets and enormous sofas. Mrs Viney, an attractive woman, who must have spent a good deal of the year sunning herself in Florida, offered us a glass of something strong. Frank got straight down to business.

"Okay, so the UNCUT diamonds (I noticed Mrs Viney blush at the mention of the word 'uncut') were returned to Cohen. Millions of readers of the National Dailys were entertained over the pre-Christmas period by your daring escapade on the Northern Line."

Mike Viney offered Frank an enormous Havana cigar and lit the tip for him.

"But, first off, (and this has been niggling me for ages) I want to know the identity of 'the friendly blind man'?" I said.

"Now't problem!" Sid by now a bit tipsy and over showy, lit his pipe and tossed the spent match into the ash-tray. "T'friendly blind man wi' ginger beard and dark sunglasses were Mike's brother, the balloonist in disguise."

Frank shook his head.

"Negative, that diamond you found some six yards or so from the ventilator, young man!"

"Warra' about it?" said the Yorkshireman, burping into his glass.

"It wasn't rough-cut, Mr Ramsbottom – you overlooked the distinct 'V' shaped indentations where the facets would have originally adhered to the crown. I should hazard a guess – the tiny sparkler accidentally detached itself from a lady's ring or brooch."

"And – who was this mystery lady?" I asked, helping myself to some Turkish Delight – being passed around, rather hit and miss I might add, from one of us to the other! That booze was high octane, alright! "Lady walking her pooch on the Heath or what?"

"Let's suppose Mike's identity was 'the whistler' and his brother kept an eye on the balloon while he climbed down the ventilator shaft to the disused station a long way below … who was this other accomplice? The so-called 'friendly blind man' who travelled on the same train as Cohen and held up the guard at gun-point with so much flair and obvious rapport with the passengers? For starters – I'm convinced we are dealing with a 'she' and not a 'he'."

"A lass!" Ramsbottom nearly swallowed his pipe whole!

"Or as Sherlock Holmes might have said if he were with us now – 'THE woman'. You know, I once saw a West End production of Bill Pastons 'Lives and Letters' at the Haymarket. The leading lady was billed as Nancy Starr and took the part of the famously forthright Mrs. M. who steals the last scene by stabbing Lord Wisley in the bath with a kitchen knife! I'd recognise that lovely face anywhere! She won the Evening Standard award for best actress and the play ran to packed houses in the West End."

It suddenly dawned on me that the walls of the living room were covered with theatre posters and publicity pictures of Mrs. Viney, the woman sat over by the piano.

"Mrs. Viney alias Nancy Starr was the actress in question. You've also done some radio and TV work I believe." She nodded.

"And it was you who mislaid the diamond".

"Yes it was." She gave her husband a sultry look and lit a cigarette.

"Aren't you forgetting something," I said, helping myself to more powdery cubes of Turkish Delight. "Let's not forget our false ginger beard, sunglasses and the mask. These items were not found near the ventilator but by a porter in a waste-bin on the north-bound platform at Hampstead Underground Station."

"And I've got a blinkin' good idea how they got there!" Frank glanced over at Viney's pretty teenage daughter. "Duplicates – that's how!" The girl started tugging at the poodle's ear. "That was a clever ruse – in fact, so darned clever it got me thinking that a fourth party was involved. What if, as pre-arranged on the evening of the robbery, Mike's daughter took the tube to Hampstead Underground station and around the time the power was cut slips a DUPLICATE ginger beard, sunglasses, bowler hat and so on – identical to those worn by the 'friendly blind man' and the 'whistler' into the waste-bin amongst the rubbish? The police would be put on the wrong track."

"Okay, but what's the motive?" Viney was now getting restless.

"That's not hard to guess," Frank grinned. "Your company is facing financial difficulties."

"That's part of it certainly, but there's more … you see, over dinner at a restaurant in Hampstead one evening, I was discussing our firm's current cash-flow crisis with my wife – when, out of the blue, Nance mentions she's got an idea for a completely 'over the top' Agatha Christie style 'whodunnit' set on the London Underground. She gave me the rough outline and I have to say I thought the plot was brilliant … not only that, but I realised with the robbery, my company would soon be financially solvent again."

"So you acted out this plot to the play in 'real life'?" Viney nodded.

"I got chatting with Mr. Cohen over the garden fence. I said I was interested in purchasing upwards of two million in rough cuts. These would end up as rings, bracelets and necklaces – sold exclusively by the

Viney-Marks Chain. I insisted he bring them to my house – it was next door to his, after all.

Sensing a deal, Cohen agreed to bring the gems to my house on the evening of the 20th. I knew the 'Bull and Bush' pub was closed for renovations until well into January and in winter that part of the heath is remote and unpopulated … also Cohen was a man of regular habits. Every evening, without fail, he would get on the tube at Holborn, change at Euston and then travel on the Northern Line as far as Golders Green. He always arrived back home at around quarter to seven – give or take five minutes.

He also preferred to sit in the front of the train. We knew this because for a fortnight, my wife and Laura took it in turns – disguised of course – to follow Cohen's every move after he left his office at Hatton Gardens."

"Aye, but that don't explain why yer gave owt' diamonds back – does it!"

"I'll come to that …" Viney relit his cigar. "The robbery was a spectacular success. We made it to the surface in one piece and while Nance clambered aboard the balloon, I replaced the lock on the ventilator with a new one. My brother piloted the balloon across the Heath and before flying on to Brighton (as planned with the diamonds) landed in the field round the back of our house used for grazing my daughter's horse … funnily enough, I remember my wife mentioned she had mislaid a diamond from one of her ear-rings. At half-past nine I was about to uncork the 'champers' when the old doorbell rang. It was Cohen! He looked to all the world like something just crawled out of the Chapel of Rest ... the last few hours had obviously been a strain. He told us he never wanted to travel on the London Underground again for there had been a robbery.

My wife poured him some strong coffee and sat him down ... he apologised for not keeping our appointment ... we would read all about it in the papers the next day, he assured us.

He was certain his Cockney clerk, Vincent Harris, hired from the Brook Street Bureaux in High Holborn had somehow masterminded the debacle ... although the police found not one scrap of evidence to support this theory. Well, Cohen went back home with his tail between his legs and Nance feeling a twinge of guilt, suggested that we'd better return the stolen gems or the old bloke might never recover.

I had also, by then, lost my nerve! I didn't fancy a long term in prison and if some clever detective from the Met put two and two together I'd be in for the high jump!

I rang my brother in Brighton and told him to stick on a false beard, wig and sunglasses and pop round to the Western Road Post Office in the morning ... get the diamonds off to Cohen's Hatton Garden address quickly.

To this he agreed.

It had been a darned good adventure anyhow, even if the old firm does go bust!"

Fred's Old Banger

One sunny morning – the bushes in the square swollen with mauve rhododendrons and children playing on the grass – mums feeding bits of bread to hungry gulls – we returned to our basement flat after flying a model plane over at Shoreham which managed to collide with a kiddie's push-chair on take off.

I was putting the kettle on for a well deserved cuppa when Frank received an unexpected telephone call on his mobile from his brother-in-law, Fred Stockley.

Fred, a retired Civil Servant who invested his life savings in a market-garden business, had this big old red-bricked house on the outskirts of Henfield.

Peculiar circumstances conspired to bring the muddled affairs of the late Morris Porrit, once Senior Partner in the Coachbuilding firm, Pinnock & Porrit (the hearse and caravan conversion specialists with a works in Worthing) hurtling into the same orbit as Frank's brother-in-law.

"Harry, Fred wants us to pop over and see him this afternoon – alright."

"Well, it's certainly the day for a nice run in the country!" I said, spooning in the thick syrupy Carnation milk Frank preferred in his tea.

"Funny, I haven't heard from Fred for ages. He was a bit 'off-colour' and kept himself buttoned up at Hilda's funeral but then, we were never very close anyway … now, let's have one of those nice jam doughnuts we got from Safeways – no point in keeping them in the bag, is there."

We puttered over to Henfield in the Bubble car and turned up just in time for lunch – cold ham and salad, followed by a punnet of raspberries – fresh from the Garden Centre.

Enjoying a half pint of stout, whilst gazing out of the window at the gravel drive, Frank said, lazily:

"I don't want to sound impertinent, Fred, but what made you buy that old hearse outside?"

"The Bingley Motor hearse – you mean? Well, that's partly the reason I got you out here. I've copped a bit of bother," – he sipped his beer. "Last year, my neighbour, old Morris Porrit, partner in the firm Pinnock & Porrit, once one of the biggest builders of motor hearses in the country, died after a long battle against cancer. In the final stages of 'Big C' he went a bit barmy – lost his marbles if you like!

After the funeral, I happened to bump into Reg Porrit, the old boy's son, walking his dog round by the village duck pond. 'Fred!' he says, looking well peeved, 'I've got a big problem.' 'Oh – what's that?' I asked, preferring to mind my own business but curious just the same.

'The company's facing financial difficulties – what with coachbuilders like 'Lockharts' flooding the market with cheap hearses from Czechoslovakia – well, I had hoped to inherit a few bob from my old man … and d'you know what that rat, Binns, the family solicitor, told me when he read out the Will – Dad apparently bequeathed me a secondhand motor hearse – not worth a bloody halfpenny! Always did have a sense of humour! I suppose it was all that morphine that turned his brain in the end.'

'Well,' I said, calling my dog to heel and patting his moist muzzle 'Put it up for sale.'

'Who the hell would buy it?'

'Hang on a minute, that Escort van of mine is on its last legs – I need something to carry the potted plants and shrubs about in – .'

'You'd better come and take a 'butchers',' he said glumly.

Well, I did pop round to Reg's place that same afternoon. The Bingley Motor hearse was just what I needed for the market garden centre. Granted, I'd probably spend most of my time under the bonnet but for a cheap little runabout – who's complaining!"

"Anyone approached you about buying it since?" asked Frank, twisting his wheelchair round to get a better look at Fred.

"Funnily enough, our village builder, Brooker thought I was desperate to get rid of it, then a fortnight ago a blonde, Marilyn Monroe type, enquired about the old hearse ... travelled by train from Brighton where her husband apparently runs a second-hand book business."

"What was she prepared to give you for it?"

"Three hundred and fifty quid. I refused of course."

"Three hundred and fifty quid?" I was amazed and could see by Frank's gormless expression that he was too.

Now if we were talking about a secondhand mini – something worth investing time and money in – I could understand – but, an old motor hearse – the world was going nuts ...

"Did she leave an address?" Frank looked puzzled but a shrewd, penetrating gleam surfaced in his eye.

"No, I honestly never thought I'd hear from or see her again, Frank."

"Well, going back to an earlier point Mr. Stockley, where did Morris Pillock, Porridge 'or whatever his bloody name is, put his money if not with the family – must have been worth a few bob, surely?" I asked.

"Bequeathed the lot to a dogs home – that's what the solicitor said, anyhow."

Fred got up from his chair and lit a cigarette.

"Come outside you lot – I've got something I want to show you."

I helped manhandle Frank's wheelchair down the stone steps.

The 25 hp Bingley Motor hearse was parked in the drive next to Fred's Escort van and his wife's Polo. We went over for a closer look.

Frank stuck on his spectacles and took out his notebook. Fred did his level best to explain what the big deal was.

"Reg Porrit told me this model was highly popular with British undertakers before the war – the first one that is."

"Would this type of hearse see service today?"

"Unlikely, Mr. Stow – what with a top speed of barely 22 miles an hour – you're joking! If you had to get to the crematorium it would be wiser to catch the bloomin' bus!"

The 25 hp Bingley Motor hearse, like all hearses of that period, was plain and functional. Knocked up out of wood with fluted glass windows – the doors hung on special hinges at the back to allow full clearance for coffins – there was a torpedo ventilator on the roof.

"There –" Fred stabbed his finger at three cross-bow bolts protruding from the mudguard, number plate and spare pneumatic tyre.

"Christ!" exclaimed Frank, trying to light his aluminium pipe and singeing his fingers with a match. "Someone doesn't think much of your bedding plants, Fred! Those high-sided doors and the windscreens don't offer much protection – do they? Whoever fired those bolts was a lousy shot anyhow."

"I collected some sacks of fertiliser and on the way back from East Grinstead I swear I never saw or heard anything remotely suspicious ... mind you, the cam shaft and pistons of the old girl's four cylinder engine makes a hell of a din. There's plenty of woodland along the lane so suppose this bastard with the crossbow hid behind one of the trees. I recall seeing a break-down truck parked in the forecourt of the 'Mill Pond' public house just round the corner from my place – but, ... it was only when I got back to the garden centre I realised what had happened ... my God, my hands were shaking so bad I could hardly hold me tea straight."

"What's that you collected from East Grinstead, Fred?"

"Dozen bags of Huntley's Fertiliser and six sacks of Fisons."

"Well, garden mould's hardly worth killing a person for! First what I want to know is – is this hearse actually one of the models designed and patented by Reg's father's company – Pinnock & Porrit?"

"Yes, I've got all the documents inside."

"I'd like to look at those presently."

Frank sat back in his wheelchair and listened attentively to the birds.

"What do you think, Frank? I'd value your opinion being ex-Flying Squad an' all – why should somebody want to murder me … a market gardener – for Christ's sake!"

The poor old chap looked anxiously at the cross-bow bolts. A gentle breeze ruffled the feathers. Frank came out of his twittering, bird-inspired reverie and took a long pull on his pipe.

"This break-down lorry you mention – taken in context with what appears (and I only say appears) to have been an attempt to hi-jack your old hearse – or, shall we say more pertinently – orchestrate a crash, seems highly suspicious." He frowned.

"Do you remember the firm – name of the garage – Fred?" Frank said, excitedly.

"The drivers cab was sort of rusty brown … British Petroleum sticker on the front mudguard and a thingy on the back with a hook on the end of it." He appeared to dither.

"Make of vehicle? C'mon we haven't got all day!" said my pal, impatiently.

"Ford – no, wait a minute, might have been a Jap. make – could have been a … oh, I dunno, sorry Frank – they all look the bloody same these days – don't they!"

I could only agree with him.

Frank puffed on his pipe. I confess the thought of this menacing breakdown truck lurking in the forecourt of the pub … with its engine ticking over …

quite gave me the 'heebie-jeebies' but who would want to hi-jack an old hearse …?

A room with a telephone was hastily commandeered, overlooking the driveway and one of Fred's nursery assistants roped in to keep an eye on the Bingley Motor hearse on the strict understanding that he should fire a starting pistol if anybody remotely suspicious were to approach it or try to drive it off.

Fred's wife, Marge, insisted we drop everything and have a cup of tea. Fred read the Mirror while I lounged on the sofa, munching digestive biscuits.

Sat over by the window in his wheelchair sifting through a pile of registration documents belonging to the hearse – an ex-Scotland Yard detective with many years' experience with the Met (before premature retirement) – my pal went about this task methodically – using a magnifying glass it took him under five minutes to discover a discrepancy …

"Harry, read this for me, will you?" he said, passing a piece of paper over to me.

Placing my mug on the arm of the sofa, careful not to slop tea on the covers, I leaned over to read the document.

"It says here – 'supplying one of the latest type Daimler ton truck chassis' …"

Frank slipped off his spectacles with the frames fastened together with Elastoplast and rubbed his eyes

"Read the whole thing – Harry!" he suggested. Unlike Frank, I've never had a very 'retentive' brain (thick in other words) and found all the blessed facts and figures difficult to follow.

Pinnock & Porrit Co. Limited
Repairs suppliers replacements
Worthing

To: Supplying one of the latest type Daimler Ton Truck
Chassis, complete with two electric head lamps driven off the
generator, two oil side lamps, oil tail lamp, electric horn, jack,
pump and tools: fitted with 29 x 440 Balloon pneumatic tyres
to the rear wheels; £112
Delivery charges from works; £5
Supplying and fitting aluminium number plates and
licence holder; £1
Supplying instead of the existing electric head lamps driven
off the generator, and oil side and tail lamp, an electric
self-starter and lighting set, including all five lamps, working
off the battery, and fitted complete with dynamo, starter,
and the necessary wiring, and, of course, tail lamp at the
rear, which for an hearse is, in our opinion, the only
method of lighting suitable; £14
1 – 29 x 440 Dunlop cover, tube and rim for the front wheel
£4.18
1 – 30 x 5 Dunlop cord pneumatic, cover, tube and rim for
the rear wheel £10.12
Constructing a Patent Pinnock & Porrit Bingley Type
Motor Hearse Body, No. 3 with patent fittings, also
HEARSE DELIVERED COMPLETE READY
FOR IMMEDIATE USE ON THE ROAD for the
sum of; £300
Total = £447.10

I took a breather and sipped my tea. Frank wagged his thumb and directed my wavering attention back to the document.

Extras if Required
Patent Pinnock & Porrit Nickle tip-up wash basin, with tank,
taps, pipes, etc.
Canopy lamp embossed on glass.
Coat of Arms if hand-painted (by transfer included in
quotation).
Painting black inside with Ripolin.

I ran my bleary eyes down the page to check I'd not missed anything.

"Now go back to the beginning ..." Frank smiled sadistically. "According to the documentation, the Bingley Motor hearse was fitted to a one ton Daimler chassis – right or wrong, Harry?"

"Right, that's what it says here."

"Well, my friend – how come the hearse out there is bolted to a modern FORD chassis frame?"

A biscuit clenched between my teeth, I congratulated Frank.

"You must have eyes like a ruddy ferret."

"How many 'phones you got in this house, Fred?"

"Let's see ..." the market gardener thought for a moment – "there's a mobile upstairs, another one in here and a third in the office – that's the asphalt-roofed shed behind the greenhouse."

"Well, we're going to be making a lot of phone calls. I must ascertain who're the authorised Ford dealerships in West Sussex. I've got a good chum, Joe Stafford, who part-owns a garage in Henfield, perhaps he might have a list? I'll ring him presently and jot down the details."

"And what are we supposed to say to the bloody dealer people, anyhow?" I asked.

The ex-Flying Squad detective, turned Private Eye, drummed his fingers on the armrest of his wheelchair and grinned.

"What was that solicitor's name – the one you mentioned earlier, Fred?"

"Oh, Binns, now I see where this is heading."

"I need to verify whether a new Ford One-ton truck chassis was ever sold to either Mister Morris Porrit, the firm of Pinnock & Porrit, or Mister Porrit's legal representative, Binns … and enquire very politely what became of it … there must be a delivery chit – some record of the transaction! We'd better find whoever fired those cross-bow bolts at your old hearse, Fred, before he decides to shoot at you again!"

Fred puffed nervously on his cigarette.

"I'm not about to argue, Frank."

Each of us, with note-pad and Biro handy, went our separate ways and after a couple of hours spent on the 'blower' ringing round various dealerships, I started to feel like one of those girls at the telephone exchange – probably started to sound like one too.

At a quarter past four, still with umpteen dealerships to contact, one of Fred's nurserymen stumped into the shed and told me Mister Donaldson wanted me back at the big house – right away …

None of us could claim much success but Frank as it turned out had made inroads.

"Radfords of Worthing!" Frank triumphantly chucked his pencil at the far wall. "Nice young man on counter service – very helpful. A Ford one-ton chassis was apparently sold to a Mr Binns, acting on behalf of a Mr. Morris Porrit – not his firm – you understand – on the 2nd of the month … that would have been roughly around the time he died … oh, and we're going to put that old death wagon of yours up for sale, Fred."

"Why not let me run over to Henfield in the car and stick an advert in the local papers – Gazette and so forth – I could even arrange postcards to be displayed in shop windows. There's just time before they shut."

"Oh, and we'd better unbolt the magnito from the hearse and put it in a safe place," said Frank, pulling up the brake handle and manoeuvring his wheelchair closer to the fresh pot of tea Fred's wife had just brought in.

The advert read like this:

For Sale
1 Bingley Motor hearse 25 h.p.
Good condition ideal for taking
Loads (1 ton).
Non-skid tyres.

Speeds Low Gear 15 miles per hour
High Gear 22 miles per hour

Callers welcome

MR FREDERICK STOCKLEY
WYMONDHANS
NR. HENFIELD

I shall also include here an accurate facsimile of names and addresses taken from Frank's notepad:

The Abbey Hotel	Tel.
Henfield Police Station	Tel.
Johnson Matthey & Company	
smeltering works Ltd	
Paul Street, London EC1	Tel.
Maw & Co. Coachbuilders	
Hog Lane	
Holborn Viaduct	Tel.

That night me and Frank slept in one of the spare rooms. It was lovely to be out in the countryside. Apart from Frank's snoring and my farting – I could hear the owls hooting. The moon shone brightly through the mullioned window but, in the middle of the night, I was disturbed by what sounded like a heavy goods vehicle thundering backwards and forwards along the lane at the end of Fred's drive.

Marge agreed to sit up all night in the front room keeping an eye on the hearse … in the morning she had nothing to report but I'm certain her being partly deaf and near-sighted didn't exactly help!

The advertisement had been placed in the Friday edition of the Gazette. The telephone number for reasons apparent later – deliberately omitted.

After breakfast, letting the grub settle, I was watching Frank and his brother-in-law playing Pool in the conservatory when Marge popped her head round the door.

"There's an enquirer for you, Fred." she shouted.

Frank, slinging his cue aside, rolled his wheelchair behind some thick curtaining and I did the same.

Fred, as prearranged, was to do all the talking. It turned out Edward Jackson, the village odd job man was the first caller of the morning. Wearing a cloth cap and grubby working overalls, his pinched face was pickled red by the wind and sun, he had been unblocking drains over at the schoolhouse that morning.

"How much do you want, mate?" He took out a cigarette and attempted to light it... his hand was trembling ... booze with a capital 'B' I thought!

"You've already got a van – what are you going to use the hearse for?"

Frank was watching the man carefully from the gap in the curtains.

"I want to strip down the coachwork for winter fuel and keep the chassis to carry logs from the wood to my yard. I've got a nice little earner on the side – making telegraph poles for BT."

"Break it up! Oh, I'm not having that! I want the hearse kept in road-worthy condition ... I'm really looking for an enthusiast to restore it."

The odd-job man looked at Fred as though he were mad – then, like some horse-trader at a fair – he took out a grubby wad of bank notes from his overall pocket

… licking the end of his thumb – he began counting them up.

"Twenty-five pound!" he proposed.

Fred shook his head

"Twenty-five fifty."

Fred still shook his head.

"Twenty-six and that's your lot, mate!"

"Sorry!" … that was final and Jackson stuffed the notes back into his pocket and left.

In contrast to Jackson – not more than ten minutes later – our next caller set the old ticker racing. She was a blonde – like maybe Monroe or Jane Mansfield – pure Hollywood dame. She wore a light summer frock, elbow length gloves.

"Nice to see you again," said Fred, holding out his hand.

"And you, Mr. Stockley." The lovely blonde slipped off her lavender-pink gloves. "I saw your advert in the Gazette this morning. My hubby said I should come over and see you." The girl smiled sweetly – "Will three hundred pounds be enough?"

"Sorry – I forget names."

"Barbara Blue – call me Babsie!" The girl took out her cheque book. "I enjoyed my little walk up here from the station. You can see the pretty gables of your house from the footbridge, did you know that, Mr Stockley?"

"Barbara – oh, Babsie, we've got a slight problem."

"If you want more money …"

"How can I put this – you see, unfortunately, the old death wagon has already been sold."

Mrs Blue or Babsie … suddenly lost something of her glamorous effervescence. She bit her bottom lip. Fred kept his cool.

"Half-an-hour ago – eh – chappie from Croydon."

"Whereabouts – ?"

"Croydon."

The blonde uttered something unmentionable under her breath which sounded distinctly like s..t!

"Name of Bloggs – manufacturer of boot-blacking. He's driving up to Croydon this afternoon … wanted me to keep the hearse while he attends to some 'blacking' business with the 'Cherry Boot' Polish Company. What can I say … tax disc, the vehicle's documents and so forth have already been exchanged."

"Well, I expect my hubbie's business can manage without it."

she said this with a solidly forced smile … glancing at the mirror and dabbing her eyelash to remove a trace of mascara.

"Have you an address I could contact Bloggs at in case the hearse comes up for auction?"

Fred shook his head. Babsie lowered those sultry eyes of hers and got up to leave.

"Good-day, Mr Stockley! I shall see myself out!"

"Yes, goodbye Mrs Blue eh, Babsie."

We heard the front door slam shut as though it had been kicked by the hind legs of a mule. Frank trundled out from behind the curtains.

"What a splendid actress – she ought t'make a Hollywood blockbuster with Mel Gibson – will you become her agent or I, Harry?"

Fred lit his fag and inhaled deeply.

"There's a girl for you," I sighed … "now, if I'd been a few years younger …!"

"She wouldn't have given you the time of day, young man!" Frank said, with a cruel laugh.

"Did you notice how her expression changed when Fred told her the old banger was sold … by Christ, she's a real little Bette Davis – that one."

I was still reeling from the scent of her expensive perfume clinging to the walls of the room, but this was no time to dawdle on matters of the heart.

Suddenly the doorbell clanged and Marge shouted from the hall:

"Billy Bishop to see you, Fred."

We fled behind the curtains. Not long after a bit of a loutish character breezed into the conservatory.

Bishop adjusted his Nike cap and grinned.

"Nice gardening centre you got here, Guvnor"

"Yes, we've built it up over the years but, presumably, it's not my garden centre you've come to see me about?"

"Saw your advert in the Gazette didn't I – and when I comes up the driveway I says to myself 'Billy Boy, I've always wanted to customise an old hearse and stick a big jet engine on the back' – out comes the parachute' – lovely!"

"And, what did you hope to pay for it?"

"Five hundred smackers – an' that's yer lot!"

Bishop admired himself in the mirror and straightened his Nike cap. Confidence oozed from every pore.

"You're very generous, Mr Bishop."

"Call me Billy Boy, guv, all me mates in Brighton do."

"Well, Mr Billy Boy, unfortunately there's a slight hitch."

"Hitch is my second name, old son! Problems! Never 'ad one in me life – neiver did me farver or me grandad before 'im."

"The hearse has been sold."

"Mr Stockley!" Bishop's eyes gleamed like a tiger's. He produced a long bladed knife from his belt and brandished it, menacingly. "I fink you an' me 'orter come to some arrangement! See, Billy Boy wants somefink – he gets it! I mean if there's a long queue at the club – what does Billy Boy do – ee goes straight to the front an' barges fru them big double doors – an' no bouncer's stupid enough to stop 'im – cause one fing people got in common is a basic instinct for self-preservation an' they don't wanna end up buried under ten foot of concr…"

"Oh yeah!" bellowed Frank, "How would Billy Boy fare in the slopping-out queue, I wonder?"

Frank, sat in his wheelchair, bore his controlled aggression well. He trundled from behind the curtain and aimed the aforementioned starter pistol directly at Billy Boy's crutch!

"Drop the blade – now – ."

The colour drained from Bishop's face.

"Drop it! You've got nil seconds on the clock, old son."

"Look here – you wouldn't dare fire that thing."

Bishop now spoke with an altogether different accent – a very posh one. His eyes never left Frank's for a second but so far as 'bottle's' concerned – ex-Flying Squad plays second fiddle to nobody!

"Wouldn't I –?" Frank grinned – baring his dingy yellow smoker's teeth like a rabid dog.

Bishop's knife clattered to the ground.

"See… I suffer from a bit of split persona myself, Billy Boy, alias Mr Cecil Bagshaw late of Johnson & Matthey Smelterers Ltd. … 'schizophrenic' is what the doctors like to call it? Part of me gets this overwhelming urge to squeeze triggers. Oh, Fred, phone Henfield Police Station and ask 'em to come out here – straight away! I had a chat with Detective Sergeant Rutherford of Sussex Fraud Squad yesterday but he may need to be updated. I'd guess you've got a heavy duty breakdown lorry parked out in the lane with the adorable Babsie sat in the front, manicuring her nails. The police, will of course impound it!"

The time for amateur dramatics was over. Bagshaw seemed more than ready to talk.

Frank wheeled his chair over so that the large wheel could crush the villain's foot if necessary.

"How did you find out about Johnson and Matthey?" Bagshaw almost choked on the words.

"Us ex-Scotland Yard detectives have a word for it – hard graft! But, it was that blunder of the modern chassis that started the ball rolling. 'Small is beautiful' Mr Bagshaw – I never tire of that phrase."

"Dear God –" Bagshaw shook his head and groaned… "you know about Maw & co. – then?"

"The specialist coachbuilders, welders and plate-makers, who, amongst other things transferred this old hearse body from a one ton Daimler to a modern Ford frame. Certainly – I am also aware that Johnson and Matthey are a city firm of smelters who deal in precious metals, platinum, silver, gold dust and bullion."

Frank paused to light his Falcon pipe.

"Yesterday I made enquiries and discovered the company Audit Office in Paul Street received an order from a Mr Binns, a solicitor acting on behalf of Morris Porrit, for gold ingots to the value of one hundred thousand pounds to be smelted and processed by that company.

The girl on the other end of the blower wouldn't disclose what happened to the gold after it was smelted, naturally that was strictly company business between the client and themselves and, to do so, would have been a breach of confidentiality.

When I rang Radley's garage in Worthing, an authorised Ford dealership, they confirmed that a one ton modern chassis ordered by Mr Binns on behalf of Morris Porrit, had been despatched to the London Company of Maw & Co., specialist coachbuilders.

It dawned on me that there could be only one feasible explanation why someone would want to hi-jack an old hearse. The hearse, or, at least, some part of it must contain something very valuable. Why was the chassis swapped ... that really got me going.

From my time spent with the Flying Squad, I have developed over the years, a cabby's photographic memory for the streets of the capital. Maw & Co. is just round the corner form the smelting works of Johnson and Matthey.

Going on a copper's hunch when I phoned the Audit Office, I put out a few leads ... had any situations become vacant recently? I was a professional smelter by trade – seeking work.

'Yes,' the girl said.

'Oh, was it Sid Weeden that chap who did electrolytic refining whose left?' I asked, casually. 'Gone to South Africa, I believe.'

'No, it was a Mr Bagshaw who everyone knew.'

He'd left a couple of weeks' back – gone on honeymoon apparently – and then she gave me a fairly good description of yourself.

Now, while I pass the gun to friend, Harry, here and refill my pipe, perhaps you'd be good enough to fill us in with the blanks – Mr Bagshaw?"

In the distance I could hear sirens – the police were coming. Bagshaw seemed fairly resigned to failure but you never could tell, for instance, if he suspected I was holding nothing more lethal than a starter pistol he might have acted very differently and got violent … very violent, indeed!

"While working for Johnson and Matthey I was refining gold by the Miller Chlorene method – the bullion work went to another part of the building. One day an operator went sick and I was asked to take his place.

I wandered over to the blast furnace and was greeted by Mr Beggiwegg, a company chemist, who – along with a chap called Binns – were to oversee the morning's work.

I was intrigued because, apart from the usual crates of gold ingots, there were some specially tooled moulds corresponding to parts of a motor vehicle chassis. As a direct consequence the front and rear axles of that old hearse parked outside the garden centre are drop-forged from pure gold encased in tubular steel … "

I nearly choked on a fruit gum.

"The frame contains a square seam of gold running throughout – as do the specially bored cam shaft, crank shaft, pistons and connecting rods – oh, and as some sort of malicious prank – Binns directed that a set of boxed tools – normally supplied standard with the chassis – should be duplicated in solid gold and painted with nickel.

During a tea-break I slipped into the office. This Binns' character's attache case lay open on the desk. Him and the chemist were busy yapping to one of the blast furnace operators. I looked inside – the briefcase contained everything I wanted to know – the intended destination of the old hearse – delivery dates – even a copy of the old boy's will. It only took me a short time to memorise the details.

Me and the missus (Babsie) decided to build a small smelting furnace in the back garden of our terraced house in Brighton. We fully intended to hijack the hearse and tow it back to Brighton. The plan was to go to Malaga and live in luxury on the proceeds.

Everything went well until we found out the hearse had been sold to a market gardener, near Henfield…

It was when I fired my crossbow at the tyres of the Bingley Motor hearse – things went badly wrong…

For starters, the hearse was going too fast. My wife should have driven the breakdown lorry up the lane and blocked the hearse off – leave Mr Stockley tied up in the woods and then we'd drive off to Brighton but, what neither of us had anticipated was the blessed breakdown lorry broke down.

I could hear the bloody engine whinnying like a frightened horse in the forecourt of the pub just round the corner.

Babsie is not mechanically minded and found it impossible to get the lorry started. There I was, in the middle of the road scratching my head, watching that old hearse King Midas should have died for, turning off into the Garden Centre.

We've been staying at the Abbey Hotel in Henfield and couldn't believe our luck this morning when we saw that enticing advert of yours stuck in a shop window... silly fool, what a bloody fine mess I've got myself and the missus into ... ah, I see the police have arrived!"

Doctor in Disgrace

The weather in Brighton was decidedly muggy. Frank was having to contend with a melting vanilla ice-cream – a large dollop of which slid down his cardigan front.

A shiny red Post Office van with its distinctive shape somewhat distorted by the glare of a shimmering heat haze, turned left at the lights.

"I'm being broiled alive," moaned Frank. "The plastic seat of this wheelchair makes my bum feel like a burger on a blasted oven-plate!"

He chucked the remains of the ice-cream away, scrubbing at the front of his cardigan with a hanky.

We crossed Western Road, about to enter the Square on our way to the sea-front café, when we heard a loud, piercing scream.

Frank rolled his head round to see what was up. A woman in a flowery frock and blouse was staggering down the steps of a cream coloured, stucco fronted Georgian Terrace.

A copper on the other side of the Square – with a quick flourish of his wrist – barked something into his police radio and started running.

"Can't you push this ruddy thing any faster, Harry."

By Christ, at times of hard graft like this, I wished Frank had invented some sort of rocketry device constructed from light alloy, to bolt onto the back of his wheelchair!

Now rolling about on the pavement, the poor woman was wracked with violent and convulsive spasms. Kicking off one of her shoes she lay still.

The heavily perspiring constable started feeling for her pulse.

"She was waving at me from that window trying to get my attention!" The copper said glumly

Frank slipped sun-shades over his spectacles and peered up at the house.

"Which window did you say?" he asked.

"Third storey – just look for the window box with the red azaleas."

The woman was dead. Her last agonies had ravaged her fairly attractive features. The eyes bulged like a seal and seemed to plead… 'Why me Lord, what have I done to deserve this?'

Frank took the Officer aside and had a word in confidence. The policeman frowned and jotted something down in his notebook.

I was staring down at the dead woman, wondering what to do next when a young man whistling an old Spice Girls hit, wearing a white open-neck shirt, navy pin-stripes and two-tone brogues, came down the steps of No. 39.

"Passed out has she – all this bloody hot weather – can't say I blame her … bit of rain's what we need,"

"She's a gonner – I'm afraid." I said sadly.

Then I noticed (with some relief) the binaural stethoscope with its flexible tube for both ears dangling around his neck and the chest-piece tucked into his waistcoat.

"So, you're a doctor, then," I said stupidly

"Good God – it's one of my patients!" He ignored me and bent over to take a closer look at her. He frowned intently at the corpse.

"What's that you say?" Frank sounded gruff and official.

The doctor pointed his thumb at the classical portico of No. 39.

"I examined Mrs Wanderslow no more than ten minutes ago – went upstairs to visit another patient, Mr Royce, who forms part of my round ... Pat was sat by her bureaux writing letters."

"What was wrong with her?" I wanted to know.

"Routine check-up," he sighed. "Apart from a little wax in the ears, she appeared to be in perfect health!"

"Well – for what it's worth – I'm an ex-nurse and ..."

"Oh, where was that?"

"Stoke-Mandeville Hospital! Mr Donaldson is a Private Detective! We formed a partnership and have a little flat in Hove."

"Oh really," he grinned. "A mate of mine, Doctor Lithgow, worked at Manchester General..."

Frank got chatting with a bronzed, leggy blonde in big sunglasses, wearing a glitzy bathing robe and bathing cap ... she had been sunbathing on the balcony next door.

The doctor and myself left the body where it was and headed for the cool shade afforded by the portico of No. 39 Berkeley Mansions – still keeping a sharp look-out for the ambulance

The policeman once more conferred with Frank. *What the hell were they gassing about* ... search me! – then he came over. The Officer was possessed of an aggressive, if controlled ambiance which made the doctor feel uneasy.

"Mr Donaldson is ex-Flying squad, I hear Sir?"

The voice had a mocking, cynical edge to it.

"Yes, him and Mr Stow here have a Private Detective Agency in Hove – why?" said the doctor guardedly.

"Because a number of jolly nice sorts from our Murder Squad will be arriving shortly. Sorry to be such a bad sport…this hot weather an' all but I'm placing you under arrest."

"Under arrest! What the blazes for?"

"Mr Donaldson, he of the wheeled chair and feathered trilby, put forward a very intriguing theory – proposes this woman died after being administered a fatal dose of poison! Funny how you were one of the last person's to see her alive and, being a G.P., doubtless had access to…"

Before our 'promotion seeking' constable could deliver his 'coup de gras' the doctor shoved him aside, leapt over the wrought iron railings bordering the private gardens – disappeared behind a clump of rhododendron bushes – was glimpsed briefly over by the phone kiosk – before merging with the crowds teeming along Western Road.

While the red faced constable blustered into his radio, a patrol car and the ambulance turned into the square!

A detective got out of the car and ambled across to where the dead woman lay – her backbone by now hideously arched.

Frank lit his aluminium pipe and watched the paramedics quickly unload the stretcher.

"What makes you so sure she was poisoned," I asked Frank.

"To be honest, Harry – inspired guesswork. The pathologist will perform an autopsy, of course. What got me thinking there might be suspicious circumstances was primarily this…

Why was she waving from that third storey window up there trying to grab the attention of that copper? Now, if she had been taken ill why not simply shout upstairs – the good doctor was attending another patient in the flat above."

"G.P.'s you never can trust 'em these days," I said, remembering the 'Harold Shipman' case.

"The doctor was in her apartment and the poison had to be administered by somebody! Listen – I've been chatting with Mrs Sieff, who was sunning herself on the nextdoor balcony. Apparently, Mrs Wanderslow lived alone. And she was a widow."

"Wait a minute – the name Wanderslow rings a bell!"

"I enjoy a cuppa, first thing – 'WANDERSLOW DIVIDEND TEA' – ."

"Come off it, Frank – you're not seriously going to tell me the dead woman's related – used to collect those Boris Karloff fantasy horror cards."

"Prefer footballers and monkeys, myself!" Frank said, with a broad grin. "Look Harry, Mrs Sieff told me the widow's husband was the tea billionaire, Isaac Wanderslow, who died in that power boat accident last year – off Monaco."

"I think we'd better take a look round her flat – third storey, you say?"

I gazed up at the building and grimaced.

We took the lift and the house porter, an aged specimen any embalmer would have been proud of, showed us to the widow's apartment. Along the corridor were traces of vomit. It turned out the woman had also puked into a metal waste-bin placed next to her writing bureaux in the living room.

The trappings of her spacious, nay luxurious apartment, were wholly consistent with a man who started life as a barrow boy in the East End of London and ended up the Chairman of our foremost wholesale supplier of bulk and packet tea in Great Britain.

Fifteenth Century Flemish gilt-framed paintings by Van Eyck and Weydon graced the walls. A Rubens took pride of place above the fireplace. There was a Baby Grand, heaped with photographs of Isaac and what was apparently his first wife lounging aboard gorgeous yachts in Cannes and Florida Keys. There was one picture of a boy taken on what appeared to be a fishing trip.

The house porter – very talkative for a corpse – told us the boy's name was Bernie, the tea billionaire's son by his first marriage… now a young man, Bernie spent most of his time hanging out with artists and sculptors in Brighton. He had a fiancee Deborah – pushy girl apparently – student at Brighton Art College.

With his hands pumping the treads, Frank reversed his wheelchair and went snooping about over by the writing bureaux. Pens and some dozen light blue envelopes lay scattered on the floor. On the flat of the roll-top desk was an opened box of Basildon Bond.

While the detectives heads were turned, Frank snatched one of the envelopes, carefully slipping it inside his jacket pocket. He checked the bathroom, scribbled a little note in his diary and sucked thoughtfully on the stem of his pipe.

For myself, I felt our Doctor had been wrongly accused of a crime he did not commit by a promotion seeking copper – but to run off like that was tantamount to getting a Life Sentence for murder – perhaps he might see sense and turn himself in at the nearest police station…or would he? I thought not!

The forensic boys and a police photographer wearing white protective gear, arrived.

Frank wanted to test his theory and the pathologist, Bill Welch, an old mate promised he would give our flat a buzz when he had finished examining Mrs Wanderslow's body over at the mortuary.

We returned to our little ground floor flat in Hove where I spent the remainder of the afternoon, despite all the windows being flung wide open…sweltering under the oppressive heat…trying to construct a 'Chesney' model of a Piper Cub powered by a four bladed prop and petrol engine.

Later, as I cooked dinner…the old brain-box cells still trying to work out how to fix *part A10032 into 263', glue along smooth edge of parts 03226, join 03228' – cut and join two halves of part IV (235) etc.* …Frank sat over by the dresser sweating like a pig in his string vest! Engrossed in some experiment – attentively brushing resin on to sheets of writing paper.

After a light meal of beefsteak, suet pud, chips and peas followed by spotted dick – submerged in thick, creamy custard, we settled down with our smokes to listen to the wireless. Barely had I twisted the dial when the old second hand Phillips set – temperamental at the best of times – emitted a diabolical farting noise.

I smashed my fist against the formica lid hoping to duff up the valves a bit when lightening suddenly flashed behind the nets and there was a rippling peel of thunder directly above the Square.

Rain started hammering against the window. I suspected few people would have the energy to be out in this kind of humid, thundery weather – and got a shock when at about half past seven I heard a girl laughing on the step and the persistent grating of our doorbell.

Stepping over Roy, our comatose cat, who had for some reason decided to hibernate on my slipper, I went to answer the door.

A young lady wearing a floppy waterproof, stood on the porch shaking out her wet brolly. I kept wondering where I had seen that face before?

"Is Mr Donaldson, the Private Eye, at home?" she asked.

There was a tremendous boom of thunder which made me jump!

A bit flummoxed, I mentioned something about the heat wave we'd been having and showed her into the living room. Frank peered over the top of his Aero Modeller magazine…a big smile crept across his face.

"Nice to see you again Doctor." he laughed, chucking the modelling periodical on to the table.

Bright yellow waterproof and brunette wig were hastily dispensed with, although despite the rugged use of a flannel, traces of rouge blusher, lipstick and mascara could only be effectively scrubbed off later with warm water and a nail brush.

The doctor – now a man again – collapsed on our plastic covered settee, kicked off a pair of high heels and with a groan massaged the ball of his foot.

"How women wear these blessed things all day – I'll never know!" he laughed. "I caught a bus along the front to Peacehaven – got this get-up in a charity shop for fifty pence and did a quick change in the public loo across the road! Got your agency address from the telephone directory."

"Your enormous feet are a dead giveaway!" Frank looked very serious. "Sussex Police have issued a warrant for your arrest."

"Oh and I suppose you and Harry here will be handing me over to the police – fair cop – well, perhaps, I did act rather rashly! I'm a bit impetuous like that but I didn't murder Pat Wanderslow and that's why I've come here tonight – someone has to bloody well believe me! Can I count on your vote?"

"Certainly," Frank nodded, lighting a Kensitas and offering him one from the packet. "Presuming Mrs Wanderslow *was* poisoned ... which reminds me, I'd better phone Bill, the pathologist, about the autopsy. He'll still be at the mortuary."

Frank leaned over his wheelchair and picked up the envelope which he had earlier retrieved from the widow's sumptuous apartment.

"And, this little item of evidence might help get you off the hook."

Frank held an ordinary light blue envelope up to the lamp. The bright light from the bulb penetrated through the flimsy paper revealing the ghostly outline of a clearly defined watermark.

"Basildon Bond!" the doctor shrugged, taking a puff on his cigarette.

"The envelope is addressed to Miss Beatrice Lorne, 'Windy Knook', Seaview Drive, Bungay, Suffolk," said Frank.

"Beatrice Lorne – never heard of her!" the G.P. yawned. "Was she the one who did away with Mrs Wanderslow…poison her – I mean?"

"You'll notice the envelope isn't properly sealed – pass it to friend Harry here and see what he can make of it?"

It was plain light-blue manilla. The folded letter inside contained a few lines about cat-litter and the regular watering of cacti plants – it didn't exactly inspire my old brain – I passed the envelope back to Frank. After watching the telly, we all went to bed.

In the morning the doctor, refreshed after a good night's kip on the camp bed in the spare room or workshop as we liked to call it, helped cook breakfast and dress Frank.

We bundled into the Messerschmitt Bubble Car and Frank drove like a maniac along the sea front to Brighton Art College. All I kept thinking was Dear Lord, I'm going to end my days smashing into the back of a bloody bus or mowing down a pedestrian or cyclist.

We tore round by the Royal Pavilion, the old Yamaha 750 cc motorbike engine screaming like a banshee, and eventually ended up (not overturning) but parking by the college building. The camping trailer in which we towed Frank's wheelchair under tarpaulin was also very handy for this type of run.

Frank had phoned Sid Ramsbottom, the 'Sherlockian nutter incarnate', earlier at his flat in Kemp Town and asked him to meet us outside the college.

Smoking a big yellow Meersham pipe, he came bounding across the road towards us – an omnibus edition of Sherlock Holmes adventures – tucked under one arm.

Wearing my old cast-offs, with traces of lipstick and mascara, the good doctor had the kind of high profile we could do without! Ramsbottom told him to stay outside – preferably behind one of the pillars with a shopping bag over his bonce!

In the entrance hall the attendant gave us all a stoney, obdurate look. He was built like a brick and reminded me of one of those propaganda posters during World War One of the Boche Square-heads charging with bayonets fixed – all he needed was the ruddy gas-mask!

"You lot from a coach outing for the disabled – then?" He went over to Frank's wheelchair and deliberately stuck his shiny shoe on the chrome footrest.

"'ard bastard!" Sid muttered between clenched teeth.

"We're looking for a student – girl by the name of Deborah – know her – do we?"

The attendant shrugged.

"So many bloody kids – I lose track of names."

Frank started to make a thorough nuisance of himself, shouting and demanding to see the Head of

Department. A member of staff alerted by all the din intervened.

Frank once again mentioned Deborah, an Art Student at the College, and this time we got a more positive response.

Sharing lift space with a trolley piled high with picture frames, we ascended to the floor above – down the end of the corridor was a Room XVII. The room was brightly lit and reeked of linseed oil and paint.

"Deborah!" called out the staff member who accompanied us. "Someone to see you."

Frank twiddled his thumbs looking at no one in particular. A corker of a brunette, wearing overalls and Doc Martins, using her brush to splodge on thick layers of oil paint, looked up.

"Yes?" She admired her painting "I asked for No.6 camel-haired brushes last week and the blasted ones they sent me were No. 8's," the girl mumbled.

"I sympathise," Frank said. "I want to ask some questions. I'm a Private Detective. I'm trying to trace the whereabouts of a certain doctor."

"Oh, him…the one the police are after…I read all about that caper in the Argus."

"You know Pat Wanderslow personally?"

"Yes of course – now, Bernie's mum Naomi rides a Honda Fire Blade and enjoys jumping off tall buildings and bridges on twangy bits of elastic – why Issac had to divorce her and marry boring old Pat instead is one of life's great mysteries."

Young madam balanced her brush on the easel, piling her chestnut curls into the most delightful little 'top-knot'. She was a good looker and knew it!

"I'm Bernie's fiancee – in case you hadn't guessed."

"Sid, may I draw your attention to that shelf next to the radiator – could you pass me that bottle with the white powder in it – see where those tubes of oils are?"

The girl was about to reach over and grab it but our Yorkshire friend, sensing first blood, held her wrist firmly and prevented her from doing so.

"Nay lass, its now't trouble, really – what would you say t'bottle contains – Vim, bleach or cocaine?"

Deborah looked decidedly peeved.

"White powder paint of course! Oh you Northerners are all alike! Faggots for brains – family works in't mill, I suppose?" She mimicked his voice.

"There's now't wrong wi' faggots young lady!"

The Sherlockian passed the tiny bottle for Frank to inspect.

"Much too crystalline for powder paint – I'd say it was more of a salt," he said, passing it on to me.

"Careful not to touch, Harry! Just unscrew the cap with a hanky and tell us what it smells like."

"Odourless – can't smell a thing."

"I had an interesting phone conversation this morning, Deborah. An old pal of mine, Bill the pathologist, performed an autopsy last night! I'll spare you the grisly details but he discovered traces of antimony – a metallic poison – more than two grains present inside Mrs Wanderslow's body."

Frank took the Basildon Bond envelope and waved the envelope in front of her face like a Chinese fan.

"As the great detective, Sherlock Holmes, might say – 'I congratulate you for your considerable ingenuity

Madam, alas, I must condone the crime!'" Frank lowered his gaze.

There was a loud bashing at the door.

"Ah, Inspector Kensit, glad you could make it… nice chat we had on the phone earlier."

"I've arrested the doctor – bloody well sunning himself in his baggy tee shirt on the College steps. Your Bubble Car's parked on a yellow line, by the way…I bribed the Traffic Warden…what are you looking at me like that for Frank?"

"Because my dear old thing you've arrested the wrong person."

Somebody tittered. I think it was a member of staff but they quickly shut up.

"I'd like you to meet Deborah who, using Bernie as an accomplice, poisoned his step-mother Pat Wanderslow! I have the evidence here."

Frank held up the light blue manilla envelope.

"Incriminating letter – eh?" said the detective. "Well, come on, Frank…read it out…we haven't got all day."

"No need – it's the envelope not the letter that interests me."

Frank unfolded the flap…

"See that fine strip of gum running along the edge that glues the flap down?"

Bill nodded… the girl fainted.

I gallantly rushed forward and being an ex-nurse did my bit to revive her. I always carry a small bottle of 'Otlays' smelling salts from Boots around with me, and this came in handy.

When she was sufficiently recovered, another member of staff helped me to lift her up onto a chair.

"Firstly Deborah." Frank continued. "popped into Smiths and bought a nice presentation box of Basildon Bond stationery. And when her colleagues were having their lunch break in this very room – she undid the box and knowingly tampered with the contents.

An art student, Deborah took a brush and skillfully applied a fine layer of antimony (an odourless white crystalline salt, soluble in water) to the gummed strip of each envelope. The solution was allowed to dry and the envelopes replaced in the box.

On Monday, Deborah visited Mrs Wanderslow's flat in the Square. Probably over a fag and cup of tea, the presentation box of Basildon Bond was placed unobtrusively on the bureaux and there it remained until Mrs Wanderslow chose to write some letters! Now what do we do after writing a letter? We slip it into an envelope and..."

"Lick it!" I said.

"Exactly Harry – Mrs. Wanderslow had written her letters, stuck them in the envelopes and unwittingly ingested the antimony by moistening the gummed strip of each envelope with the tip of her tongue... but, by the twelfth – the one I'm holding here…she felt the beginnings of acute stomach pains and nausea.

The astringent, metallic taste in her mouth and burning in her throat would have been most unpleasant. She staggered into the bathroom, vomited over into the basin with its gold taps and then returned to the living room and paused over by the window. A copper (an ambitious one) was on the other side of the Square.

She was by now desperate to attract his attention and waved frantically…you see, Pat Wanderslow knew who had poisoned her alright.

Deborah banged her fist against the easel.

"Pat was a silly bitch who only ever cared about one thing. *Supporting good causes* – giving all her money away to charity – buying silly hospital equipment like kidney dialysis machines or air ambulances. What good is SERIOUS money to a person like that! Bernie and me were going to SPEND the lot – get through millions like there was no tomorrow! That stupid cow would have lived for ever! They always do, these goody, goody two-shoes! You've ruined everything Mister Big Shot WHEELCHAIR MAN –" She spat at Frank.

"Young madam'll get pair o' rubber knickers t'wear when they 'ang 'er!" fumed Sid in a blast of nostalgia, forgetting that the likes of Calcroft and Albert Pierpoint no longer plied their trade with the rope and they didn't hang women in this country anymore. "Thou'll be in fer t' drop."

"Stick that famous envelope of yours into a forensic bag, Frank! Our boys will want to analyse it –c'mon you!" he said to the girl.

"Let's find out where your nice fiance Bernie lives."

"Not forgetting t'bloody antimony!" The Yorkshireman jabbed his finger at the Windsor & Newton screw-cap bottle.

One of Inspector Kensit's colleagues took care of it.

Our 'Deb's Delight' was about to enter the Poisoners Hall of Fame. Frank prised open his tobacco tin and filled his pipe.

"You know, I remember reading in the paper how the tea billionaire bequeathed his entire fortune to his second wife, Pat. Presumably if she died it would all go to charity – mind you, he must have resented the way in which his step-mother was made the sole beneficiary!"

"So would bloody I!" Ramsbottom was emphatic – he struck a match to his Meersham – "Specially when'tits all goin't end oop wi' Oxfam or some flippin' Missionary Society – that's crunch! Bye gum I'd tear me 'air out thinkin' 'bout al't them do-gooders queuein' up for hand-outs wouldn't you Harry – billion quid…we should be s'lucky."

Jingly, Jangly Jackdaw

On New Year's Day, a couple of years after the fateful armed robbery in Tulse Hill that left my pal, Frank Donaldson, then a Scotland Yard detective in the famous Flying Squad with men under him, crippled for life – paralysed from the waist down by a bullet lodged in the base of his spine – I was pushing his wheelchair along the sea front not far from the little ground floor flat we shared in Hove.

I first met Frank when employed up north as a male nurse in the Orthopaedic Wing at Stoke Mandeville Hospital. We were both recently widowed and, by some strange quirk of fate, shared the same hobby – a love of flying Radio controlled model aeroplanes, the type you construct from bits of balsa wood, glue and resin. I might add, Frank also had a wide experience of mechanical engineering and designed many pieces of ingenious apparatus for his personal use…and in the field of criminal investigation that often comes in very handy.

Despite sporadic scatterings of cinders, the pavements were icy and treacherous under foot. It had started sleeting and there was a fierce wind blowing off the sea…much to our amusement, for mirth has a warming way about it, an old gent was toddling past the shelter unfurling his umbrella with the greatest difficulty – trying to operate the switch on the handle – when, due to a particularly strong gust of rain, wind and sea water, the shaft tore away from the bamboo handle.

We watched, amazed, as the top half of his brolly took off, twirling into the air and hurtling towards us like a gigantic, flapping bat. It came crashing down and proceeded to skid along the pink paving stones.

Frank, having the time of his life, tore after it in the wheelchair, sliding all over the place like a rally driver. He managed to trap the brolly beneath the alloy foot-rest and energetically rolled over the thing a couple of times – presumably to kill it!

"Why, thank you, Sir," said the old chap as he came puffing over from the sea front shelter.

"You'll have to get it repaired," I said. "There's a 'quick-fix' place along Western Road – d'you know it?"

"I'd better throw the thing away," he frowned, examining the twisted spokes and rent canvas – "but, I am extremely grateful to your friend here. I should not have fancied being taken to court over the loss of an eye, or worse…by the way, does either of you gentlemen live in Hove?"

"Yes, we do – whose place are you after?"

"I'm searching for a Mister Frank Donaldson, a retired Scotland Yard Officer who operates a small private detective agency hereabouts. Miss Mimms, a member of our local Bridge Circle who used to live with a Mrs Cooper in a flat above a shop in Lancing by Sea – 'A PURVEYOR OF LADIES CORSETRY AND BRASSIERES' – recommended him to me."

"Harry Stow – glad to make your acquaintance!" I said, shaking his hand. "It so happens – Mister Donaldson's the very same bloke who attempted to rescue your brolly."

"Good gracious," he sounded well relieved. "My name's Reginald Smythe and I am a retired accountant from Marine Drive."

"Well, Mister Smythe," Frank replied, throwing his knitted blue and white Seagulls scarf across his shoulder and releasing the brake handle – "I hope I can be of some assistance. The number's 23A – just across the road in the square…coo – real brass monkeys weather, this – that's right Harry – give us a shove!"

Smythe was a likeable enough character. He had that dignified, reserved manner of the ex-city man…hardened by and slightly cynical from decades of commuting. Bright green eyes held you in a steady gaze and a resolute, chisley chin spoke of a life-time spent appraising accounts ledgers and company balance sheets.

Once back at our flat, Frank settled in front of the gas fire, and while I put the kettle on, listened with 'pricked up ears' as Smythe explained why he had bussed over from Marine Drive to seek our advice.

We were a bit low on the old money so anybody's fee would be welcome – I thought it might be a lost cat or a budgerigar needed finding but I was mistaken!

"There has been a New Year's Eve burglary, Mister Donaldson…unfortunately, several of them."

I nearly dropped the teapot on the floor.

"And, you were one of the casualties?" said Frank, taking out his aluminium pipe from his cardigan pocket.

He nodded.

"But, I have no inkling how the thief actually broke into my bungalow and still less….how he managed to get away with it! The matter doesn't rest there, however, because this morning I received a summons from my neighbour, Philip Lamb, the retired bank manager, only to discover that his bungalow had been burgled and he, in turn, had been informed on the blower that the house opposite, belonging to Stanley Rogers, the headmaster of the College, received a dose of the same."

"What got stolen?" I shouted from the kitchen, turning up the gas.

"Jewellery! My wife lost her diamond necklace and several rings – none of my stuff was touched and this proved to be the case with Lamb and Rogers."

"Did you call the coppers?"

"Wha – pardon, my hearing aid keeps picking up Southern Counties radio – if it were Classic FM I wouldn't mind so much."

"Did you call the police." Frank shouted.

"No, I'm afraid not – we don't want our names in the papers and all the fuss of having to go to court."

Rogers and Lamb felt the same sense of foreboding... the matter has not been discussed outside our circle. We celebrated the New Year with Hattie, our dog, and Mr Matthews, our manhelp. At a quarter past one my wife went to bed.

I was about to join her but thought I should remind Mr Matthews, a sincere and obliging chap – if a bit doddery and altogether one of the most sensible domestics we have employed, that the window in the living room required battening...shortly after, my wife nearly screamed the house down."

"And, where did your wife keep her jewellery?"

"In her dressing table."

"And, I suppose it was unlocked?"

"Well, I mean a lady does not expect to have her boudoir broken into!

Now it was still extremely cold outside – I remembered no snow had fallen since the previous afternoon. Thus, after comforting my wife and leaving Hattie with her, I decided to take Mr Matthews – together with a torch and search every inch of my property. I was determined that if the thief had left behind any tell-tale evidence of his night's work I should be the first to know it…

Outside, the sparkly crust of snow running along my garden wall remained intact – obviously no one had attempted to clamber over it."

"Highly perceptive of you," Frank said, with a boyish grin, squeezing open a tin of tobacco and filling his pipe bowl.

"Oh, since childhood I've had a real passion for crime fiction Mister Donaldson, and hoped I might be able to put the knowledge gained to good use.

Anyhow, the lawn was covered with a foot of snow. All I could see from its glazed surface were the prints of my dog's paws and my wife's galoshes leading up to the bird-table. Mr Matthews, I think, had ventured along the path.

I then turned to face my bungalow to check if the window ledges had been disturbed – if a ladder had, perhaps, been leant against them or the gutter – the layer of snow was unbroken. We do have a ladder with two stages of rungs and nobody had touched it."

"Well, we have three bungalows close to each other – granted 'New Year drinkies' allow a certain amount of lee-way for the burglar, but you mentioned you kept a dog, Mister Smythe?"

"Indeed, we all do," he said brightly. "My spaniel barks at the slightest noise! Stanley Rogers keeps a black labrador...Lamb, a collie."

"Well, I'm buggered!" Frank leaned forward in his wheelchair, picked out a biscuit from our tin and dunked it into his tea. "Marine Drive – that's a No. 25 bus – isn't it?"

"Oh, any running along the seafront usually gets there!" said our client, taking his cheque book out of his pocket. "Of course, on New Year's Day there are a lot fewer buses."

Frank loved to drive our specially adapted Bubble car, and with me stuck in the back and his collapsible wheelchair folded neatly beside the seat.

Smythe lived in a bungalow not far from the golf course. I'd say the area was fairly well-to-do, with most properties belonging to retired accountants, stockbrokers and the like.

While showing us the places belonging to Philip Lamb and his neighbour, Stanley Rogers, the old chap pointed out that each had been designed as part of a development project by the quirky Scandinavian architect, Svenson, and this accounted for the peculiar pot-pouri of styles.

For instance, the front of Smythe's residence reminded me of an Alpine hunting lodge, whereas, his neighbours bungalow incorporated the traditional

Finnish log-cabin façade – many timbers and shuttered windows.

The wintry weather suited them wonderfully and in this snowy landscape, one could quite easily have been about to test the slopes of the Tyrol or encounter a herdsman with his reindeer.

We met the 'missus' standing under the porch with her dog. Yap-Yap-Yapperty-Yap-Snap-Snap! It just wouldn't stop barking…the bloomin' noise it made. We were shown into a large, airy drawing room, comfortably furnished with a nice fire.

"How kind of you to come," said Mrs Smythe, helping Frank off with his coat – the dog was growling at me – baring its teeth!

"My trinkets, I suppose, would fetch little at auction but I attach great sentimental value to them. None of it could ever be replaced. Jo Lamb is heartbroken – her diamond engagement ring and a pair of her mother's matching ruby earrings have been stolen, but, why Mister Donaldson, should this thief leave behind my husband's wallet containing money, his gold Rolex watch and his cuff links? There was also some valuable silverware."

My pal smiled thinly and lit his pipe, tossing the spent match into the ashtray.

"Perhaps, our invisible man was only interested in sparklers…easy to get rid of."

"Why, I had never thought of that!" said the woman, picking her dog up and hugging the little beast to her bosom.

"A jackdaw of sorts?" I mused.

"Oh, that's good, Harry!" said my pal, with a chuckle, manoeuvring his wheelchair so he was facing Mister Smythe on the sofa.

"Let's have a 'butchers' at that bungalow across the road. Have you a torch…don't worry about this!" He indicated to the queer contraption resting in his lap – "It's a periscope attachment with an unusually thick and extra powerful reflector glass – I use it all the time…telescopic – you see…."

I had to laugh. Frank was fascinated by anything mechanical and spent many happy hours in what we fondly referred to as 'the workshop' – a cramped back room of our flat which had been converted for building our model aircraft or ingenious pieces of mechanical apparatus – his electric wheelchair, with all 'mod cons' (powered by an old lawn mower engine) being a prime example.

"I shall get Mr Matthew to fetch a torch," the retired accountant replied.

Once again, simplicity and utility were evidently in the architect, Svenson's mind when he designed the Lamb's bungalow, for it could have passed for a Customs Post on the Swiss frontier. Interestingly, it possessed a high shelf or platform on the roof…apparently once designated to become a glass-domed observatory which, according to Smythe, never saw the light of day on account of its prohibitive cost and the widespread criticism the project received from neighbours in Marine Drive.

Great gangly, icy spears hung from the guttering and the glow from the horn lantern made the snow shimmer like glitter dust.

Philip Lamb, the Headmaster, answered the door in his dressing gown. He was a grim, skinny individual, with swept-back silvery hair and thick lensed specs.

"You are 'the' Mister Donaldson…I take it?"

"That's me – this is my good mate, Harry Stow – your wife took things rather badly, I hear?"

"I'm afraid that is the case…look, my hearing aid is out. Are you coming in or what? Josephine is presently practising Chopin for a W.I. concert in the Drawing Room…so you shan't disturb her –"

"Oh, no bother, I'd like to take a look round the side of your bungalow if that's alright with you, Mister Lamb?" Frank shouted at the top of his voice.

"Surely you're not suggesting this thief managed to scale the wall – that's preposterous!"

"I doubt whether our thief changed into a blue-bottle, Mister Lamb, although I grant you he certainly has a most ambidextrous mind – if I were you, I should shut that door, you'll catch the death standing out here."

There was a granite path leading round the dustbins and Frank took full advantage of the fairly bump-free surface, pausing here and there to minutely examine a drainpipe or sill.

"I don't have a spirit level handy but what do you make of that window over there, Harry…here, I'll shine the torch on it for you."

"Both sliding sections of the frame don't run true to the sill."

"Yes and the bathroom window frame is only lightly pinned in and should lift away easily from the wall with the aid of a chisel. You can see how the lime-based mortar was not mixed properly and the brick-nogging around the window needs repointing."

"Thanks to the British workman, our house-breaker has no need of a glass-cutter – he simply removes the entire bloody panel…"

"Assuming the bathroom window is not fixed in properly we might just conceivably be talking about a suitable means of entry – a bloody long shot, I know – but, the tellys would have been blasting out and they're probably all deaf."

Frank rubbed his mittens together and blew out some freezing air from his lungs.

"Mr. Lamb wears a hearing aid as does Mr. and Mrs. Smythe and the dogs would be quite sleepy. But three bungalows burgled in one night and, anyhow, the dogs would have surely gone bonkers – I can't understand it…?"

Suddenly, the bewildered expression on Frank's cherubic face changed to one of wicked glee…

"Well, I'm buggered – I think our jackdaw is about to have its wings clipped!"

He screwed a tiny spade attachment to the tubular steel telescopic arm he always carried around with him…extended it and scooped up some snow from a gulley in front of the drain.

"And – there's the bloomin' evidence –" he chuckled. "Come on, Harry, give us a push back to Smythe's place – I'm dying for a cuppa."

"Do you know of Richard Jenson, the entrepreneur and businessman?" said Frank, warming his hands in front of the fire.

Mister Smythe thought for a moment:

"Do you mean the dare-devil chappie?"

Frank nodded.

"Not personally, although I believe he is something of a celebrity Brighton-way and lives on the sea front – faddish place – looks out on to the shingle beach."

"I would like to go and pay him a visit!"

"I think you will find him away at present in Tunisia…working on a pop video," said Mrs Smythe, patting her dog.

"Something in The Argus?"

"Yes, according to the paper, Jenson will be out of the country for several weeks."

The Bubble car tore through the traffic lights – Frank being colour-blind failed to stop on red – several cars hooted.

My pal couldn't care less…he had a bee in his bonnet about something and just looked straight ahead…

"Steady, Frank!" I said…

A piece of hardened fibreglass resin fell off the door where I had fixed a draughty hole.

"What has Richard Jenson got to do with all this?" I shouted from the back of the Messerschmitt Bubble car.

"He is a keen pilot and flies both helicopters and fixed wing aircraft. 'Out of the country' indeed – tut tut, I think we shall find him much closer to home."

"I suppose he'd get a couple of thousand quid for robbing those bungalows if he's lucky…that is."

"Oh he's got plenty of lolly."

"Then, what would be his motive?"

"Excitement – what else does a man with everything crave?"

"Look Frank, he might be made of money but robbing people for the sheer sport of it is immoral."

"Is it – try telling him that."

We parked along the windy promenade. Lights were on in Jenson's beach house. Frank wheeled his chair furiously along the granite path leading to the porch.

A burly figure in a woollen jumper emerged from the shadows.

"Is that Richard Jenson I have the pleasure of addressing?" said Frank.

Sure enough, the chap with his brush of blonde hair and nordic beard approached us. Two large dogs circled about his feet…their eyes glinting menacingly.

"Yes what do you want, if it's money you're after – forget it – there's a dozen people representing good causes and 'Housing for the Homeless' charities called this evening – try Fat Boy Slim further up."

"Money's not the issue – I've come about a burglary in Marine Drive," said Frank, adjusting the hand-brake of his wheelchair.

The entrepreneur's jaw dropped.

"You're not the police…"

"No, we are not."

You should have seen the relief on the chaps face.

"I think you'd both better come inside."

With the help of his wife, we carried Frank up an icy flight of steps and were led into a warm, spacious, art deco room, filled with the pleasant pong of cigar smoke. There was a pine table heaped with business papers.

He poured us a welcome glass of the strong stuff and lounging in front of the fire with his dogs, said matter-of-factly:

"You might not have noticed but I possess a number of glass-sided cabinets containing brass models – supplied with working parts and built by my grandfather – mostly for exhibitions. There is an American Wild West locomotive and a Merryweather Pump Engine. Place a penny in the slot and the wheels start spinning round or a piston-rod gyrates back and forth."

The dogs lay stretched on a rug watching Jenson with gleaming, baleful eyes, by the light of the flickering log fire.

"Ingenious," Frank admitted, "but I have no pennies and besides, more pressing matters must needs be seen to – !"

"What are your names, by the way?

"Frank Donaldson," replied my friend, "and, this is Harry Stow."

"Well, why waste your time and mine by coming out here to accuse me of some silly burglaries?"

"Burglaries…did I mention more than one…I don't believe I did," said Frank.

"Oh, I read about it" he answered in a slovenly way, believing we were by now both the worse for drink.

"Might have been the Gazette?" I suggested slyly.

"Yes, of course, my memory's a bit dodgy – you know?"

"That's bloody peculiar because the robbery was deliberately kept out of the papers and no article appeared in any of the local ones. Should I call a 'spade a spade' Mr Jenson?! We've come here to your sea front house tonight because I know you are a thief…admit it…you've already made a prize blunder."

"Nonsense!" replied Jenson, sullenly.

"And, what's more – I've got the evidence here to prove it."

Frank manoeuvred his wheelchair behind the sofa, placed his hand in his duffle-coat pocket and retrieved a damp ball of melting snow which he carefully sifted through his chubby fingers.

"Engine oil – wouldn't you say, Mr Jenson?"

The entrepreneur's oodles of confidence suddenly evaporated as he slumped back on the sofa.

"One of your tanks was most likely damaged when you and your pals cut engines and glided onto the roofs of the bungalows…Harry, come over here by the window – will you – I've got something to show you."

Tied to the veranda pole was a MICROLITE AIRCRAFT – the canvas cover flapped violently in the wind being blown off the sea.

"Masterly – if Charlie Peace were alive today, I'm sure he would play his violin for you, Mr Jenson!"

"I'm glad you both seem so cheerful…I'm wondering whether my little adventure hasn't turned a trifle sour but I'm damned if I haven't met an equal in you! Tell me – am I for the 'chop' or what's it worth to you and your buddy here to keep the police out of this…I am wealthy enough to give you a nice fat envelope each – no – what about a fine terraced property in Kemp Town or a cruise to the Bahamas?"

"You are acquainted with the Scandinavian, Frederick Svenson, I take it? The Architect responsible for the Marine Drive Developement."

"Ah, I see where this is leading – yes, he works for me from time to time – our new offices in Hollyrood Park, for instance."

"And, I recall you collaborated together on the much criticised Stenback Opera House in Helsinki?"

"Fredi owns a Ferro-concrete bungalow at the western end of Lake Utsjoki. I stayed with him there when I was financing the opera house project and it was while enjoying a Finnish bath that he slung a tub of water over the hot stones and told me matter-of-factly… 'Well, Rick my man,' he boasted – 'all my bungalows are burglar proof', for he employed a system of shutters and locks and catches manufactured to his own specification.

I warned him not to underestimate the British criminal class for invariably their motto was 'where there's a will, there is a way' but to a perpetual egoist like Svenson – this was tantamount to being challenged to 'fisty cuffs'.

He immediately laid down 'odds' and hefty ones they were too – that nobody could possibly break into those places without blowing them up with semtex. Being partial to a bet I decided to have a go, myself.

How to overcome the problem of locks and latches…on my return to Brighton, I paid a visit to the building firm of White & Perry who originally carried out the work and managed to obtain some useful information.

Over a cigar and a hefty bribe, Perry, a neighbour of mine, showed me the plans and pointed out that in order to cut corners and thereby make an enormous profit – amongst other areas of skimped workmanship – certain if the windows were not provided with outer-shutters nor were the frames, to his knowledge, ever set properly into the wall.

The unique pitch of the roofs and, in one case, the redundant observatory platform, was to make the task of burgling the bungalows much easier than I had at first envisaged!

Svenson would never part with his money easily and one of his impossible provisos stated that the burglary must take place when the houses were occupied and the second – that all three should be burgled together!

The more I thought about it the more depressed I became and then I struck on the bright idea of useing the lads from my Microlite Club, over at Devils Dyke. Flying had always been a passion of mine and I thought, perhaps, with room to manoeuvre, we might conceivably vault over the trees, land on the roofs and carry out a series of burglaries simultaneously, avoiding the myriad hazards awaiting even the most 'spring-heeled' of house-breakers.

The last week in December I faxed Svenson and arranged to meet him here at my house on New Year's Eve. He accompanied me on my criminal escapade as overseer to make sure 'fair play' was in order, and, as a consequence departed for Ostend this morning with his tail between his legs – a million pounds the poorer – having lost his wager."

"And, presumably, you were going to make a return trip to return the stolen jewellery?"

"Exactly…not wishing to tempt fate a second time I should have landed on the golf course and legged it across the road from there to Marine Drive.

I have in my safe three packets – each containing the missing jewellery. I fully intended to leave them on the doorstep – to be reclaimed by the occupants, but the weather worsened and we had to call the whole thing off."

"While I can, undoubtedly, appreciate your steel nerves and tenacity in aspiring to the 'perfect crime' you certainly failed to appreciate the feelings of others."

"Don't for God's sake inform the police, Mister Donaldson!" said the entrepreneur woefully, realising, for what must have been the first time, the full gravity of the situation.

"Not likely, " said Frank, "although it would be prudent if we returned to Marine Drive…let the ladies be your 'judge and jury'."

Jenson visibly paled.

"Very well – if it is to be a 'petticoat court' I must face…then so be it. I should prefer to take my chances there than with a real one."

"The recovery of their stolen jewellery and an extremely large donation to a favourite charity might swing things in your favour.

I shall, of course, attend the hearing with Harry here, who I can vouch is a very lenient judge of character."

Death on the Rocks

A holiday from undercover work and the day-to-day running of a small Detective Agency in Hove – what better than to spend a couple of weeks in August at that glorious Cornish sea-port town, well known to artists and popular with holiday-makers, St. Ives.

Me and Frank Donaldson had rented a modernised holiday flat with lift, overlooking the sunny harbour and quayside, with its golden bay.

I was sunning myself on the dazzling white balcony, sipping a Martini with Mabel, our lady-help, when the door-buzzer rang. There was a youthful looking chap wearing a grey belted mackintosh identical to Frank's.

"Could you tell Mr Donaldson that Inspector Clark from the Devon and Cornwall Constabulary would like a word – Clarkie – if yer will – he'll know who I am."

"How on earth did you find us?" I wanted to know.

"Rang your agency in Hove. Cleaner gave me your holiday address in St. Ives…you're Harry Stow, I take it, Frank's partner in crime –" he laughed.

"You'd better come in," said Mabel, smoothing her housecoat.

"Dave, old son," Frank called from the balcony. "Promoted – I hear – do they pay you better down here than at the Met?"

"Oh – farthings – listen, Mr Donaldson, sorry to interrupt your holiday and all that caper but something's cropped up."

"What's that – then?"

"Dead bodies found on a beach not far from here by some old deck-chair attendant who keeps going on about a bell ringing – they're a pretty fine mess – the Police Photographer and a team from Forensics are over there now – fancy a butchers?"

"Yes – why not! Mabel you stay here, love! Harry and myself can handle this – do some shopping – get your hair done!

Drug trafficking – an accident…any yachts gone down for instance?"

"We've checked with the coastguard. Nothing there, I'm afraid."

It was fairly breezy as we drove along the northern stretch of coast in our Bubble Car.

On one side of us lay steep cliffs and sandy inlets – the sea stretching as far as the eye could see. Shoreward – we were greeted by a primitive landscape of furze and heath and the odd retirement bungalows or isolated cottage.

The road swept round to Withypool Point – a sweep of beach with a lighthouse planted on a narrow outcrop of rock…a solitary 'Cyclops' blinking forever out to sea. The area was given mostly over to the gulls.

Marring the tourists view somewhat, were the police officers and forensic boys gathered on the beach. Three ominous heaps lay face down amongst the rock pools.

Parking the Bubble Car directly behind a Devon and Cornwall Scene of Crime van, we bustled down a granite ramp to the beach.

"Hello there," cried the Detective Sergeant – a tanned chappie with shirt sleeves rolled up.

He greeted us with a burst of Cornish amiability.

"Hey-ho Clarkie – 'nother fine day! Quite a little party we're 'aving."

"Yes, some of these chaps are not from the Coroner's Office. Detective Sergeant Bowlin...may I introduce Frank Donaldson, my old boss at the Met and Harry Stow – got a Private Detective Agency down in Sussex."

The detective eyed us somewhat suspiciously.

"Foreigners eh – well, you'd best come 'un have a look 'un bodies then."

He showed us across the sands.

"Old deck-chair attendant – Rowse – found 'em washed up on the rocks this mornin' like a lot 'un ruddy beached whales – keeps goin' on about a bell… gawd, we'll have bus loads 'un holidaymakers comin' t'gape from St Ives."

I could see our bodies further along the beach. Police Officers in white protective suits were trying to erect a screen but the stiff sea-breeze was hampering their efforts.

Spumes of frothy spray rose into the air and crashed along the shore.

We ambled across to where the first of the three bodies lay. Sergeant Bowlin frowned and kicked away a large, round pebble – crabs were very much in evidence.

"This one's obviously male – rigor's well set in – you listening Clark...see how the hair's closely cropped like a convict."

The face of the corpse was bloated and tinged a bluish mauve colour. The eyelids swollen, giving the appearance of a dozing insect. The left leg was missing and the right arm torn off at the shoulder.

"The fish have been at him – sharks I expect," Frank mumbled, taking out his magnifying lens and without sentimentality, wrenching the arm of the corpse. He examined the palm of the hand "Grazes, cuts – dirty fingernails – come into contact with chemicals."

"Yes, I'd go along with that." Clark said, "…but – what about this, Frank?"

Sergeant Bowlin helped turn the body over. There were lash marks across the buttocks.

"These marks were caused by a cane or whip of some kind – the poor bugger's been flogged!"

"Haircut strikes me as institutional," I said, but thinking of David Beckham of M.U. it suddenly dawned on me that the close crop look was in fashion with top sports and movie stars and everyone else nowadays.

"Immersed under water for some time," Inspector Clark pointed out.

"I'd say we're dealing with a kid – no more than fifteen!"

"Astute observation," agreed Clark. "There's old St. Caspars School along the coast from here at Culbones Cove."

"The deck-chair attendant mentioned something about a bell…"

The sergeant frowned.

…"Locals say old Rowse lost 'un few marbles – some say 'ee be mad, Sir."

The stiff inshore breeze was becoming stronger, waves congregated and crashed around the lighthouse. I could see the old deck-chair attendant hanging about by one of the Police Landrovers. A fishing trawler was chugging out to sea from the harbour.

Frank thought long and hard.

"I'd like for us to check out this Saint Caspars," he said, gravely. We got going.

This was not a populated region of Cornwall, the wild, shelterless landscape dotted here and there with derelict chimneys and the ruins of old engine houses.

The sun blazed down as our Bubble Car headed round Culbones Cove, the old Yamaha 750cc engine straining at the leash and we got our first glimpse of the old school. A granite and slate Victorian building with pitched roof, barred windows, a bell tower and tall chimney stacks. It looked like something out of that old black and white film 'Rebecca'.

Screeching gulls circled above the gate-house.

We came to a standstill and parked in front of the school gates. A sullen looking bugger, in a grey suit, wanted to know what we were doing there. "Let's go undercover." suggested the Inspector.

"Your business?" he demanded.

"One of your boys is ill," Mr Clark shouted. "I've brought the doctor to see him."

The heavy wrought-iron gates squealed open and we were allowed to pass through.

"What a doddle," I said, changing gear – "Old misery guts thinks we're here on medical business!"

"These places are so bloody vast that no one really has any idea of what's going on or who's coming and going," said Clark, peering out of the cockpit.

The Bubble Car lurched round the corner and I parked it brazenly beneath an imposing entrance porch. We went and waited in front of the big rivetted double doors...I tugged the bell-pull.

A shutter snapped open. A pair of beady eyes peered suspiciously out through the grill.

"Who is it – laundry?"

"Brought the doctor with me," said Clark, stifling a yawn. "One of your kids got pneumonia...we've got a fresh oxygen tank."

"Oh, that'd be Wilberforce," came the grumpy reply. "First-Former – attempted to slice off his fingers last week and eat them."

The vast cathedral-like doors squealed open and we were ushered inside. The nauseating reek of school dinners (boiled cabbage and mutton) pervaded the place.

"Ah, now I am reminded, Mister Clavering mentioned something about a specialist opinion being required. It is supposed the boy's wounds became bacterially infected by the common house fly of which, I regret to say, we have a great surfeit, at present due to the exceptionally humid weather...I shall take you to see the Head straight away."

"Good idea," said Frank, trundling along in his wheelchair.

"Here, this way if you please, Sirs...Matron's busy at present. A surfeit of nose bleeds, certain of our prefects are allowed to wander about. Pay no heed if we encounter them – they are usually quite jolly but can become a trifle dangerous as far as us normals are concerned."

'Normals' – that was us I take it!

We were shown along a labyrinth of corridors smelling of wax floor polish and walls painted a sickly duck green colour and the floor covered with miles and miles of the same shiny red dappled lino.

Doors led to various school rooms. A cleaning lady with a cart was doing her rounds.

We encountered a grinning kid in a blazer with green scabby skin whose hair appeared to have fallen out poking his tongue out at us. Our teacher, far from disciplining him or becoming heavy-handed, simply clicked his fingers in front of the boy's face and said in a dull monotone:

"Rutherford – behave."

The lad went away grinding his teeth.

"Oh, our boys are wonderful star turns…well, most of the time," the teacher chuckled.

We stood in front of an imposing brass plaque which read:

HEADMASTER S. CLAVERING M.Sc. Ph.D.
PRIVATE – NO ADMITTANCE

The door was ajar…

"Yes – what is it, Workington?"

"Gentlemen to see you, Sir."

The teacher, suspecting nothing was amiss, hurried off and left us to it.

Still working 'undercover' which I thoroughly enjoyed – we kept up our pretence and entered the Head's study. I cringed at the rack full of springy canes and leather straps…freshly oiled.

The head looked up,

"May I ask what you people are doing here?" he wanted to know… "How did you get in here – my school is out of bounds to all but staff and pupils."

"Ah," Frank said, feigning embarrassment, "I thought you would have been notified! Did you not get our letter – then?"

Clavering looked puzzled.

"I'm afraid I'm not with you?"

"School Inspectors!"

The Headmaster's jaw dropped…he snatched a cigarette and lit it.

"Perhaps there's been a major cock-up – you do have a Science Lab at the school?"

"We do!" Clavering answered, obviously with a sense of relief. "But you should ask Mr Bridge, the Biology Master, to show you round…the facilities are excellent."

"Well, that was what my letter was about," said Clark. "We want to look over the labs – make sure they're up to scratch."

"I see – well, no bother!" said the Head, irritably.

"It was all in our letter – you see – " insisted Clark.

"Yes – never mind the letter – look, I can give you half-an-hour! You will be able to make an inspection of our labs…perhaps, at a later date I can arrange with our Biology Master for you to come over and spend more time here at Saint Caspars."

I gazed out of the barred window at the rough waves battering the coast – plumes of spray rising into the air.

"Now, as you will no doubt appreciate, we have a large number of children – some of them with behavioural problems under our supervision. To stray from the Science Block precincts would be unwise."

Clavering pressed a buzzer. The door opened and another teacher stepped forward. This one was bald and very fragile looking.

"Mr Rogers, take these gentlemen to the Science Block. They are to stay for no more than half-an-hour and after that time you will escort them safely back to the House gates…is that clear!"

"I will – Sir!" the other answered.

"You understand me – ?"

"I do, Mr Clavering."

The Headmaster then turned to us once more…a certain amount of disdain in his voice:

"I trust your return journey shall not be hampered by intemperate weather, gentlemen – summer storms are renowned for their severity in these parts!"

We were taken directly to the part of the school where the Science Block was situated. Shockingly there were some empty coffins propped up against the wall – a transit van parked some distance away.

"You needn't stick around," said Clark, sensing the teacher's impatience. "We'll be alright – we'll have a quick look around that's all…just to check everything's up to A-Level scratch –"… "A-Level –" the teacher looked momentarily phased.

"Well," I said once he'd gone. "What are we bloody well standing here for…?"

"I'm going to have a quick look around the place," said Frank. "If anybody wants to know where the bloke in the wheelchair is – tell 'em I've gone in search of the 'Gents'…I should be about five minutes – no more."

"Thanks a million!" I said, taking out my fags and offering my packet to Clark. "How long do we have to keep up this 'undercover' caper?"

"Just shut up – I won't be long."

Frank went tearing off in his wheelchair while Clark and me smoked our cigarettes and soaked up the grim atmosphere…the ghosts of old Maths Teachers came back to haunt me. How many times had I been caned…over a dozen times…I supposed – less so for the strap.

Clark also seemed uncharacteristically uneasy – no doubt remembering his own school days!

"Come on, Frank!" I muttered under my breath. "Bloomin' well hurry up and let's get out of this dump."

I was becoming decidedly jittery when the doors bashed open. It was Frank.

"So – what's up?" I asked.

"Someone at the school is a qualified pilot – there's a Cessna-Pup and a fuel Hauser parked under tarpaulin over by the Laundry Block."

"Can't be all bad…how the hell can a teacher afford a swanky aircraft for his own private use?" I said, sounding somewhat mystified.

Frank looked grim –

"Let's get back to the Bubble Car…I've got a lot of serious thinking to do."

On our way over to St Ives we stopped off at the beach and had a chat with Rowse, the deckchair attendant.

"The tollin' o' the bell sur – when the ships get wrecked and go down – thems ghosts o' drowned men wha' peal that ole bell – sur!"

The deckchair attendant wandered back and forth along the beach occasionally staring out to sea as though keeping a kind of lonely vigil.

I sat for a bit in my shirt sleeves stewing in the rays from the sun, listening to the restful ebbing and flowing of the tide…suddenly my holiday idyll was rudely interrupted by the distant sound of a bell – it kept up solidly for a couple of minutes but I quickly resumed my sunbathing and thought no more of it.

We got back to the holiday apartment for a lobster salad and glass of stout but Inspector Clark interrupted our meal with some urgent news.

"We've checked the licence No. of that Cessna-Pup – it belongs to Clavering of all people – and guess what – he's got an off-shore account and also dealings with a Swiss Bank! There's something decidedly fishy about this – !"

"Agreed," said Frank, finishing off the bottle of Pale Ale.

"Lots of money being generated – but what line of business generates it – we'd better get back to the school sharpish – I've got an old copper's hunch…what's that place nearby used for – ?"

"That's the old Landscombe Mine..." Clark sounded uneasy. "That place hasn't been operated for fifty years or more...they closed it down – terrible safety record."

"Well, let's have a butchers at it." So we did.

A three ton van rumbled across the scrubland followed by a procession of at least a hundred kids carrying torches – dressed in grubby overalls and some with wheelbarrows and others, pulling camping trailers. They certainly seemed a bit subdued but happy, nonetheless.

Some had thinning hair but many were prematurely bald...why? Stress at school...overwork, bullying! I just didn't know but then a bell started ringing.

"They're headed for Culbones Cove." Clark was as amazed by what he saw as we were!

A Launch laying at anchor was waiting to come in.

"Talk about organised crime," Frank remarked. "What a rust-bucket – yes, see the green lamp flashing! It's going to dock alongside that makeshift wharf!"

A tractor-crane rumbled into view. Once the Launch had docked frenetic activity began. They started unloading drums of something or other...loads of them.

Then it suddenly dawned on us what those drums contained. 'SERIN' – what old Sadam dumped on that village, loads of the stuff – leaking toxicity everywhere.

"They're using the old Landscombe Mine as a toxic waste dump – it brings tears to my eyes to think how much money they must be making from each shipment of toxic muck. Those schoolkids must have a share in the business and be making a small fortune."

Clark adjusted his binoculars.

"The old Landscomb Mine – who'd have thought it – the whole bloody school's in on it – teachers and pupils alike!"

"Right young man – those bodies you found on the rocks were probably *radioactive* – there must have been an underground explosion of some kind, when they were storing the last batch of drums down the mineshaft."

"Yes…but, there's a terrible price to pay…" I said. "They must have been assured by the shippers that this stuff was safe but, by the look of some of the kids, I'd say they've caught a strong whiff of enriched uranium rods…which is unlikely to have done them much good!"

Well, to put it bluntly, the old launch was later impounded out at sea and its crew were arrested by Police and Customs Officers. Clavering was also brought in for questioning about illegal dumping of hazardous waste.

Inspector Clark seemed well pleased with the outcome, anyhow…as for us…we intended to enjoy the rest of our holiday far away from the glare of media interest. The Devon and Cornwall Constabulary could take all the credit for a job well done and, as far as we were concerned – they were bloomin' well welcome to it – we had had more than enough excitement for one week.